W9-CBD-681

Tie Me Up, Tie Me Down

Novellas by

Sherrilyn Kenyon

Melanie George

AND

Jaid Black

An erotic adventure in which three women discover
that sometimes passionate encounters are hotter
when there are strings attached. . . .

TIE ME UP, TIE ME DOWN
is also available as an ebook

OTHER EROTICA ANTHOLOGIES FROM POCKET BOOKS

Big Guns out of Uniform
Four Degrees of Heat

Tie Me Up, Tie Me Down

Sherrilyn Kenyon

Melanie George

Jaid Black

POCKET BOOKS
New York • London • Toronto • Sydney

POCKET BOOKS, a division of Simon & Schuster, Inc.
1230 Avenue of the Americas, New York, NY 10020

This book is a work of fiction. Names, characters, places and
incidents are products of the author's imagination or are used
fictitiously. Any resemblance to actual events or locales or persons,
living or dead, is entirely coincidental.

"'Captivated' by You" copyright © 2005 by Sherrilyn Kenyon
"Promise Me Forever" copyright © 2005 by Melanie George
"Hunter's Right" copyright © 2005 by Jaid Black

All rights reserved, including the right to reproduce
this book or portions thereof in any form whatsoever.
For information address Pocket Books, 1230 Avenue
of the Americas, New York, NY 10020

Library of Congress Cataloging-in-Publication Data

Tie me up, tie me down / Sherrilyn Kenyon, Melanie George,
  Jaid Black.— 1st Pocket Books trade pbk. ed.
    p.cm
    Contents: "Captivated" by you / Sherrilyn Kenyon — Promise me
forever / Melanie George — Hunter's right / Jaid Black.
    ISBN: 1-4165-0159-2
    1. Erotic stories, American. 2. Abduction—Fiction. I. Kenyon,
Sherrilyn, 1965- II. George, Melanie. III. Black, Jaid.

PS648.E7T54 2005
813'.01083538—dc22   2004042389

First Pocket Books trade paperback edition February 2005

10 9 8 7 6 5 4 3 2

POCKET and colophon are registered trademarks of
Simon & Schuster, Inc.

Manufactured in the United States of America

For information regarding special discounts for bulk purchases,
please contact Simon & Schuster Special Sales at 1-800-456-6798
or business@simonandschuster.com

CONTENTS

"CAPTIVATED" BY YOU

Sherrilyn Kenyon

CHAPTER ONE

*I*n her life as a covert agent, Rhea Stevenson had done a lot of things she hated: cozy up to cold-blooded killers, make goo-goo eyes at drug lords, pretend to be a Russian mail-order bride, walk unarmed in a low-cut, almost nonexistent dress into a nuclear arms deal.

But nothing in all her years as an agent had ever prepared her to do . . .

This!

"You want me to do *what?*" she asked Tee, the managing director of the Bureau of American Defense, or BAD as it was known to most of the people who worked there.

A shadow antiterrorism agency that most of the country didn't even know existed, BAD had a lot of "interesting" people in it, and Tee was definitely one of the more colorful characters. At five feet even, Tee shouldn't have been intimidating at all, and yet the small, beautiful Vietnamese-American woman held a look to her that let anyone know she was far deadlier than any cobra.

And she was.

Tee gave her a flat, emotionless stare. "You're going to be a dominatrix."

Rhea couldn't do anything more than gape as she heard male laughter from the desk in the office cube across from hers.

Her gaze narrowed as a bad feeling came over her. "And whose bright idea was this?"

Ace rolled his chair back so that he could look from the entrance of his cube into hers. He smiled at her like the Cheshire cat.

"Oh, no, no, no," Rhea said firmly as she handed the file folder back to Tee. "Not on your life. Let Agent Hotshot over there go in with studded leather and whips. Then the deviants can hang together."

Ace, who really was sexier than any man had a right to be, gave her a hot once-over. "I can't, love. I don't have the ass for it. But you on the other hand . . ." His dark blue gaze dipped down to her hips and his smile turned lecherous as if he was imagining cupping her derriere.

Rhea wasn't sure what she hated most, the boldness of that look or the way her body reacted to it. And yet her body always betrayed her with this man. She'd never understood how a woman could be both repulsed and turned on at the same time.

Surely something was seriously wrong with her.

"Is this not sexual harassment?" she asked Tee, even though a part of her was humming in excitement. "You know, I do have friends in the EEOC."

Tee looked rather amused by her question. "'Well, in this

case, Ace is right. We need a female agent to pose, and Ace thought you'd be the best one for it."

Rhea directed a gimlet stare at him. "I'll just bet he did."

Ace got up and sauntered toward them to stand in the cube's doorway. At six-two, he towered over Tee. The look on his handsome face was that of a kid at Christmas. An image that was helped by his tousled, dark blond hair and teasing, blue eyes.

He cast a devilish grin at Rhea. "Ah, just think, Rhea. You . . . me . . . chains and whips . . . Recipe for a hot night, huh?"

Recipe for a disaster in her opinion. "Recipe for a nightmare, you mean. I wouldn't do this for all the money on the planet. Sorry, Tee, get yourself another agent for this."

Tee sighed irritably. "We need you, Rhea, you're the only one in the home office who fits the profile. Put aside your personal distaste and work with Ace just this once."

"I am not going to take my clothes off around him even if I do get the benny of beating him."

Arching a brow, he folded his arms over his chest. "But would you do it to stop a known terrorist?"

Rhea paused at his words. That was her one hot button, and everyone in the agency knew it. They just didn't know why. The reason was private and personal, but she had spent her entire adulthood on a crusade to stop such needless violence. That one word could get her to do anything.

Even take her clothes off around Ace Krux, male god, personal demon.

"That's another reason we thought you would be perfect," Tee said solemnly. "We all know how you feel."

No, they truly didn't. Rhea took the file back. "Do I have to work with Ace?"

Tee shrugged. "It's his baby. He's been working on the case for a year now and knows all the ins and outs."

"Don't worry, Rhea," he said. "You'll feel differently after you see me naked."

She snorted at that. "Yeah, someone remind me that I better bring along gallons of Pepto-Bismol, an industrial bottle of Tums, and some bicarbonate."

Ace rolled his yes. "Yeah, right. Like you wouldn't sell your soul for a shot at me."

Rhea pulled her weapon out from the holster at her back, then ejected and checked her clip. "You got that much right." She slammed the clip back in and switched the safety off. "You want a ten-second head start or can I just shoot you now?"

Tee shook her head at Ace. "Why must you always torment her? One day, she really is going to shoot you and I just might authorize it." Tee turned back to her with a warning stare. "Put it away, Rhea."

Grumbling, she reactivated the safety and complied.

"Ah, she wouldn't shoot me anyway, Tee. She's just covering her infatuation for me by being a hard-ass."

Rhea stood up to confront him. "You know, Ace, you're not nearly as irresistible as you think you are."

"Sure, and just how many times have you dreamed about having me naked and in your bed?"

Rhea counted to ten in her head and forced herself not to rise to his baiting. But the worst part of it all was that he was right. She did find him physically attractive, but the minute he opened his mouth, she wanted to gag him.

"Oh, yeah," she said sarcastically. "You set my entire world on fire. Oh, baby; oh, baby. I must have your hot bod. Why don't we just strip naked and do it right here in the cube?"

Hunter Wesley Thornton-Payne stuck his handsome, albeit pompous, blond head up over the wall of the cube beside Rhea's. "Jeez, people. Could you cut the crap? You know some of us are actually trying to work over here."

"Since when do you work on anything other than your stock portfolio, Payne?" Carlos Selgado asked in his accented voice as he popped up over Rhea's other wall to glare at Hunter. "Some of us are enjoying the fireworks."

"My name is *Thornton*-Payne," Hunter corrected.

Ignoring him as he always did, Carlos looked over at Tee. "If Rhea is really going to get naked, can I bump off Ace and take over his case?"

Tee gave them all a withering glare. "Agents, down, or there will be a vicious virus that attacks the payroll system and locks you all out of the loop. It's called the Pissed-off Tee Virus and it could make it so that none of you get paid for at least six weeks . . . maybe more."

Carlos and Hunter immediately vanished.

Tee turned back to Rhea and Ace. "You two, play nice."

Rhea scoffed. "Play nice? I'd rather pet a scorpion, barehanded."

That devilish grin returned to Ace's face as he raked her

with an appreciative stare. "I'll show you my stinger if you'll show me yours."

She screwed her face up in disgust. The man was truly a reprobate.

"Hey, Carlos," he called, "you used to do a lot of work with scorpions. How do they mate, anyway? You know they got those stingers and claws and—"

"Enough with the mating rituals of scorpions," Rhea said from between clenched teeth. "Why don't we discuss the praying mantis instead? You know, the female rips the head off the male. She's a wise woman."

Ace wagged his eyebrows at her. "Yeah, but what a way to go, huh? If you've got to die, it's always best to go out with a good bang."

Tee cast a withering stare at them. "Yo, Marlin Perkins and crew, let's get back on topic here."

Ace leaned nonchalantly against Rhea's desk and folded his arms over his chest. "Okay, we'll get back on the subject now and save the banging for later."

Rhea just continued to glare at him. This was one of those times when she really hated this man.

But then Thadeus "Ace" Krux was a man of many talents. He could scale a building in a manner to make Spider-Man proud. He could drive better and faster than Jeff Gordon and Mario Andretti combined. He could construct a lethal bomb from an empty Coke bottle, a piece of tissue, and simple household cleaners.

Most of all, he could render any woman on the planet speechless at first glance.

It was a hell of a combination that was deadly to any woman's defenses. He had the sleek, seductive movements of a beast in the wild. The smile of Don Juan and the intelligence of Einstein, all of which was packaged into the body of a Bowflex ad model.

He was the epitome of everything she found desirable in the male species. . . .

And everything she despised.

His calm, cool, rationality bordered on dispassionate. His arrogance knew no bounds, and his ego . . .

Someone really needed to take him down a few notches.

Since he seemed to live for no other purpose than to torment her, he was completely distracting to her peace of mind.

"So has she racked him yet?" Joe asked as he joined them.

Barely in his thirties, Joe was young to hold the position of senior director for such an important agency, and yet Rhea couldn't think of anyone more suited to controlling the motley, often illegal bunch that made up the BAD task force.

For all his youth and handsomeness, Joe was even more lethal than Tee. He never compromised, never took prisoners. Something that was at odds with his pretty-boy features.

He had on a black leather shoulder holster with the ivory handle of a .38 Special peeking up (Joe had once said he liked being cliché on the surface), but it was the stiletto he kept strapped to his calf that he was most famous for using (that was for the surprises he liked to give after someone mistook him for cliché).

His shoulder-length, dark brown hair was worn in a ponytail, and for once he had the sleeves of his blue dress shirt rolled up to show off the telltale colors of the dragon tattoo he had on his left forearm—a remnant Rhea had once been told by Tee of the days when Joe was a member of a vicious New York street gang.

"Does this mean I have your permission to rack him?" Rhea asked Joe.

Joe gave Ace an amused smirk.

Ace snorted. "I don't think so. Remember, I do know where you live and sleep."

"Yeah, but not even you could get past my security system."

Joe was probably right. His specialty was wiring and demolition work. He could booby-trap just about anything. It was a special talent that Rhea couldn't imagine a New York City boy acquiring legally.

"So who are we after, anyway?" she asked, opening her folder.

"Lucius Bender," Ace said. "Ever heard of him?"

Rhea nodded. Of course she had. It was a case she'd been begging Joe for, and why he'd assigned it to Ace she couldn't imagine. She was twice the agent he was. At least she was when it came to research and reconnaissance. When it came to physical case execution, Ace had her beat only because the man had a flagrant disregard for human life, especially his own.

"He arms a lot of the West Bank terrorists," she said.

"Yeah," Ace agreed. "I've been aching to nail this bastard

since I worked for the Secret Service and one of his flunkies made an attempt on the president's life, but he's slippery as hell and we haven't been able to pin anything on him. The IFT just told us that a few days ago the German authorities picked up his favorite dominatrix, who they've had under surveillance for contraband. Now the brothel she worked in is looking for a replacement."

"And I'm the replacement?" Rhea asked.

Ace nodded.

Joe reached into her folder and pulled out the most recent photo of the bald, unattractive, middle-aged man for her inspection. "The GA have a bug in Ute's cell where she's been talking with other cellmates about Bender's odd habits. Seems he likes to talk a lot during his beatings, and one of the things he brags about is how many terrorist acts he's either funded or committed. He has a thing for women who look like Bettie Page, so we want to send you in as Latex Bettie, his newest toy. You go into a wired room, get him to confess, and then we come in with the GA and arrest him."

It sounded simple enough. Too simple in fact, and nothing was *ever* that simple.

"All I have to do is beat him?" Rhea asked suspiciously.

Joe nodded.

"He's a real fucked-up bastard," Ace said as he showed her another photograph of Bender at a party with a dark-haired, Bettie Page–looking girl who couldn't be any more than fifteen . . . and that was stretching it.

"Okay. If this will get him off the street, then hand me the thong and stiletto heels."

"You're killing me, Rhea," Carlos said from the other side of the wall.

Rhea huffed audibly at the comment. "Go to work, Carlos."

"Joe?" he called over the wall. "I want a transfer to Ace's case."

"Why, Carlos?" Joe asked. "You aching to wear high heels and a woman's thong?"

"Hell, no."

Rhea cleared her throat to get Joe's attention. "So how do we prep this?" she asked.

Ace smiled. "Me and you are meeting with a coach to learn about bondage and dominance. You're going to be the mistress and I get to be your slave." He looked to be enjoying this way too much.

"You really are a perv, aren't you? Admit it?"

Ace laughed.

Joe rubbed his head as if they were starting to give him a migraine. "Since the two of you are going to be extremely intimate over the next few days, why don't you leave early and have dinner together tonight so you can discuss the case and get to know each other before you actually get naked."

Now she was the one developing a migraine at the prospect of what this assignment entailed. "Thanks, Joe," she said sarcastically.

"Anytime, Rhea. Hell, I'll even let the two of you put it on the company card."

She gave him a droll look. "You're just so damned generous."

Ace indicated the way to the door with a tilt of his head. "Are we taking him up on it, Rhea?"

Rhea took a deep breath as she fought an urge to run in the other direction, but this wasn't about her and Ace and his obnoxiousness. It was about stopping a cold-blooded killer who didn't care whom he hurt.

For that, she was willing to do anything. Even put up with the most arrogant male in existence.

She looked at Tee. "I do get to beat Ace, right?"

"He'll be your slave for training. I say make him cry for mercy."

Ace looked completely undaunted by the prospect. "Beat me, hurt me, call me Ralph."

"Yeah, call you Ralph. I'll be lucky if I don't 'ralph' from the sight of you naked all right."

"Ooo," Ace said in an appreciative tone. "Swift on the uptake, Stevenson. I'm impressed."

Before she could respond, Ace returned to his cube and grabbed his jacket. Rhea went ahead and shut down her computer while Joe headed back to his office.

Tee opened up the folder again and sorted through the papers until she found one in particular, which she handed to Rhea. "This is the dossier for Bender. Memorize it while you learn to beat the crap out of him."

A distinct, evil glimmer in her eye said Tee would enjoy being in Rhea's position. "If you want this so badly, why aren't you doing it?"

"Because he doesn't have a thing for short Vietnamese women. Wish that he did though."

"Me too. The thought of going in, in nothing but a teddy doesn't appeal to me."

"Don't worry. We'll cover you."

And they would too. BAD always took care of her own. "I know."

Tee stepped back as Ace rejoined them.

"You two have a nice night and get friendly." Tee handed a small business card to Rhea. "First thing in the morning, I'm having the instructor meet you at your house where I'm sure you'll feel a little more comfortable. In the meantime, I want you two to get into character early. This is the address for an adult store here in Nashville. Head over and stock up on toys."

Ace gave that wicked grin of his as he gave Rhea a once-over that made her stomach tight. "I'm definitely *up* for it."

Rhea was completely unamused by his humor. "You better be *down* for it."

She took the card from Tee, then looked up at Ace. "You are really enjoying this, aren't you?"

"Absolutely. So what's first?" Ace asked playfully as he took a step toward her. "Dinner or sex?"

"Excuse me?"

He took the card from her hand, letting his fingers brush hers in a warm caress, and smiled like a wolf in sheep's clothing. "C'mon, Rhea. Have you ever been to an adult store before?"

Hardly. Kinky sex had never appealed to her at all, and she'd heard enough tales from her odder friends to know she had no interest in haunting adult stores for the aids they provided. "Have you?"

He looked completely unrepentant. "I'll plead the Fifth to that."

"I knew you were a pervert."

"Hey, it's not my fault the customers took me along whenever my dad made them watch me."

Rhea shook her head as Ace stepped back, then led the way from their offices toward the elevator bank.

Ace's father, Alister Cross, was a renowned director who had won several Academy Awards. Ace's grandfather, Osker Krux, owned one of the largest movie studios in the world, and Ace's younger brother was an Academy Award–winning special FX guru. Ace himself had once been a stunt double before he'd gone on to work for the Secret Service.

"You know, I've never understood why you're a BAD agent anyway. Why didn't you follow your family's business?"

He shrugged. "Movies are boring. Actors are fake and I figured if I wanted to live my life on the edge, I might as well be doing it for real. Why take a chance on dying from a blank gone bad when I can dodge real bullets intended to kill me and save the world?"

In a weird way that made sense to her, and she actually managed a grudging respect for him.

"What about you?" he asked as they waited on the elevator. "What made a respectable CIA agent follow Joe to a shadow agency that has no known ally?"

"I respect the hell out of Joe and Tee and their agenda,

and I didn't like all the rules of the CIA." That's what BAD was best at. No rules to bind their hands. Each agent was licensed as a civilian contractor. They were funded under the Treasury Department and hidden away as a federal insurance agency, which in an ironic way they really were. Only "insurance" took on a whole new meaning for them.

In reality, they were an antiterrorism special task force that no one other than the president knew about. The individual agents answered to Joe, and he answered to the head man alone.

No one else knew they existed and they all liked it that way.

The elevator doors opened.

Ace stood back to let her enter first. She didn't speak again until they were enclosed inside and he'd pressed the button for the lobby.

"Besides," she said, continuing their conversation, "I like the different kinds of agents we have. You guys are a lot more fun than the other agencies."

He laughed at that. "Yeah, we're not your average crew."

Rhea smiled as she watched Ace from the corner of her eye. Even though he worked her last nerve into an apoplexy, she had to admit he was incredibly sexy standing there with his hands in his pockets while he looked up at the floor numbers overhead. Something about him was absolutely irresistible.

Too bad he knew it.

His presence was mammoth in the elevator, or then

again, anywhere. He was one of those rare men who possessed an aura that was intense and all-encompassing.

As much as she had tried to stay angry at him for his pomposity, there had always been a tiny part of her that was attracted to him. A really *tiny* part.

When he was silent and serious, he was actually breathtaking, which had always made her wonder just how many hearts he'd left broken.

"So tell me, Ace. When was the last time you went out with a woman on a date?"

He looked at her. "A real date or an I'm-pretending-to-be-someone-else-and-am-prying-you-for-information date?"

"A real date."

He let out a low whistle. "Probably a year. What about you?"

She sighed wistfully at the painful truth. "Three years, at least."

"Yeah," he said with a sigh. "Our job doesn't exactly lend itself to dating, does it?"

"No. I'm never sure what to say when they ask me what I do for a living. Most guys are heavily intimidated by the thought of dating a federal agent."

He snorted at that. "I tell women I'm a federal agent and they laugh and think I'm handing them a line. So I usually make up bullshit about being a salesman or something."

The door opened. Rhea walked across the lobby as she continued to smile while thinking of Ace in a bar with some giggling woman who had no idea just what the man was capable of. He was incredible in the field. He could speak a dozen languages fluently and held no fear of anything.

While in the Secret Service, he'd been shot three times and had brought countless criminals to trial. She was actually amazed that Joe had been able to pry Ace loose from their clutches. He'd been a celebrated hero to his group.

"You want to ride with me?" he asked.

She shook her head vigorously no. "You can ride with me. I've seen the way you drive."

"What?" he asked, his face a mask of innocence. "I have a perfect driving record."

"Only because you charmed your way out of the last three tickets you got," she reminded him.

"Those were minor speeding offenses."

"Sure they were. And I'm a three-armed alien."

Her words seemed to only amuse him. "Fine, Cha-Cha. You drive."

She frowned. "Cha-Cha? As in Shirley 'Cha-Cha' Muldowney?"

"You know racing?" he asked as if surprised by her knowledge.

Rhea nodded. It wasn't something she ever really mentioned to anyone, but then the topic seldom came up. "Are you kidding? She's the first and only female Top Fuel Champion in NHRA history. When I was a kid, I wanted to be just like her when I grew up. My father was an old friend of her crew chief Connie Kalitta, and I actually have her autograph. Oh, I love that woman!"

"Then why is it you now drive like an old lady?"

She scoffed at that. "Old lady, nothing. I can J-turn a bulletproof Lincoln limo with the best of them."

Ace chuckled at her reference to agent training where they all learned how to handle a variety of vehicles under stressful circumstances. One in particular that all BAD agents had to pass was the ability to jump into anything available and drive it out of any possible danger including heavy artillery fire, grenade and bomb attacks.

He leaned over and whispered in her ear, "You still drive far too cautiously for my tastes."

Rhea shivered at the unexpected sensation of his breath on her skin and did her best not to think of other, much more intimate things that would cause him to be so near her.

And she had the distinct impression that he wasn't really talking about the way she handled a car.

Unwilling to go there, she led him to the parking deck where she had her red Mustang parked.

Ace didn't say anything as they got in and headed out.

"Do we really have to go to the sex shop?" she asked, even though she knew the answer.

"That depends. You got any whips and chains at home? And if you do, I will definitely have to change my opinion about what Agent Rhea Stevenson does on her days off."

Rhea groaned. "The only chain I have is the small gold one around my neck, and as for whips . . . Do half-empty containers of Cool Whip count?"

"It does for what I have in mind."

She let out a tired breath. "Does everything I say to you have to do with sex?"

"Since you're supposed to dominate me, baby, yeah."

Ace watched her stony face while she wove her way through traffic in a much more sedate way than he would have.

Rhea was a hot woman with a cool exterior that he'd wanted to melt for quite some time. But then business and pleasure didn't mix well. He knew that better than anyone and yet he couldn't help wondering what the petite brunette would taste like.

What those lean, supple limbs would feel like wrapped around his.

She was beautiful. Not so much in her looks, but in the way she could make him feel better by doing nothing more than smiling at him. She was extremely quiet and seldom said much even when her phone rang.

While in the CIA, she was supposed to have been one of their best field agents.

But in the last three years since BAD had come together, she hadn't taken many field assignments. Most of her work was done online, making Ace wonder what she'd be like undercover.

In more ways than one.

He'd always had a theory that silent, quiet women were much more uninhibited in bed. But since he hadn't known that many who were quiet, he'd never been able to test his theory.

She glanced over at him. "What are you thinking?"

Ace fell back into his standard male reply. "Nothing."

"Nothing? Then why do you look like the cat eyeballing the canary?"

He gave a wicked grin at that. "Okay, so I was thinking of you dressed in black leather, wielding a whip over my naked ass."

She didn't look at him as she made a left turn. "I think I like 'nothing' better."

"Excuse me?" he asked, stunned and excited at her words. "You really *want* to whip my naked ass?"

"No!" she snapped sharply. "I said I like 'nothing' better, not I'd like nothing better. Oh, jeez, Ace, grow up!"

He continued to smile at her, which was something he didn't do around many people. There was just something about her that attracted him against all common sense or reason.

Not even he fully understood his incessant need to tease her. Other than the fact that he thoroughly enjoyed her snappy comebacks and the way those brown eyes would flash at him whenever he made her angry. It was almost as sexy as foreplay.

Almost.

"I figured you would, which is why I said 'nothing' to begin with."

She slid a censoring look to him. "I can't believe I'm going to do this."

"You? I'm the practice slave. I think if anyone should be embarrassed, it should be me."

Rhea glanced at him as she pulled into the parking lot of

the large blue building covered in triple *X*'s that had no windows whatsoever. "Look, Ace, it's your home away from home."

Rhea stood in the doorway of the adult novelty store as total horror engulfed her. She'd never seen anything like this in her entire life. Cages were set up in the corners with mannequins dressed and chained in the most sexually graphic manner imaginable. Did people really use this stuff?

She paused next to a display of penis-shaped suckers and scowled at them.

"What's wrong?" Ace asked as he brushed past her into the store.

It was all she could do not to gape. "Where do I begin?"

He shrugged nonchalantly as if missing her point. "Well, we could begin with one of the swings over there."

Rhea couldn't help gaping now as he pointed to something that looked as if it had come from the planet Porno. The large, black contraption held a spread-eagled female mannequin completely subdued and gagged.

Yeah . . .

Unwilling to let him know she was bothered by it, she quickly recovered her facial expression and paused at the display of leather blindfolds and masks that were covered in spikes.

"Can I help you?"

Rhea actually jumped at the sound of the shaky female voice behind her. She turned to see an elderly woman with white hair and black-rimmed glasses staring at her. Jeez, it was someone's grandma! She even had the black SAS shoes and a white dress with little, dark blue flowers that matched her dark blue sweater. She looked kind and frail.

Why on earth would she be here working as a porn store clerk?

"No. Just . . . looking."

The older woman laughed and lightly patted her arm. "This must be your first time, sweetie. Just relax and have fun. Don't let me worry you, I've tried most everything in here, so if you have any questions, please let me know."

"Um . . . yes."

Grandma smiled as she watched Ace. "Well, you're a lucky woman to have that for a playmate. Why, he's simply delish."

Delish? Grandma knew *delish*?

Okay, I'm in an episode of Twilight Zone *with Grandma as the zookeeper. Just go with it, Rhea.*

Grandma continued to study him. "You know, he reminds me of my dearly departed Herbert. Oh, hon, he was the best. He just lived for sex. Would throw himself into it anywhere, anytime. In fact, we once got arrested for indecency on a subway while we were in New York."

This was way too much information.

"Have you two been arrested yet?"

"No," Rhea answered quickly and honestly. At least she hadn't been. With Ace . . . well, she wouldn't make a bet on it.

"Then you two ain't doing it right." Grandma winked at her.

Grandma was without a doubt the most frightening thing in this store.

"Oh, you'll like those," Grandma said to Ace, who had paused two aisles over. "The strawberry are the best, though my Herbert liked the lemon-flavored."

Rhea looked to find Ace examining packages of edible panties. She inwardly cringed as he inspected them. "Don't even think it, Ace."

He held up one of the packages. "They have grape." Then he looked to Grandma. "You ever try these?"

"The grape isn't the best. They have a bit of a bitter taste to them."

Ace put them back. "You said to try the strawberry?"

Rhea's gaze narrowed as he picked up a package. Fine. Two people could play that. "You also have whips, right?" she asked the woman.

She nodded.

"Do you have nice, spiked ones?"

"Absolutely, sweetie."

"No!" Ace said, putting down the panties and moving back toward Rhea. "No spiked nothing."

She arched a brow. "I can't believe I've finally found something to make the big, bad Ace craven. What on earth could make you fear spikes?"

"A Goth girlfriend in high school who left lasting scars on my flesh. I don't ever want to cozy up to another porcupine as long as I live."

Rhea was amazed he'd admitted that. "You went out with a Goth chick? How unlike you."

"Not really. I always had a thing for women in leather." He looked meaningfully at a mannequin dressed in an extremely revealing leather corset that left its breasts bare except for two tiny leather pasties.

The expression on his face said he was picturing her in that getup.

Rhea decided to play fire with fire. Determined, she walked over to the rack of leather Speedos, which would have to be laughable on any male no matter how sexy or fabulous he was. She picked up one that was of a thong design and looked back at Ace, who grimaced.

"Trust me, baby, that would be like trying to cover two bowling balls with a slingshot."

"Oh, that's disgusting!"

He flashed her one of those taunting smiles. "But it makes you curious, doesn't it?"

She hated to admit it, but he'd won this round. "No, it just makes me pity whatever woman ends up permanently shackled to you. Do womankind a favor, Ace, get neutered."

"Oh, no, honey," Grandma said. "No one should neuter something as fine as him. Take my word for it. I've seen lots of handsome men in my day, but yours . . . He's definitely worth keeping around."

"See, she likes me."

Rhea bit her tongue to keep from saying Ace should train Grandma for Bender. But rule one was never to disclose an agent's mission to an unknown no matter how harmless he or she appeared. Words could kill even faster and more effectively than a handgun.

Rhea took a deep breath and looked around. "So what appeals to you, Ace?"

He picked up a jar of chocolate body paint that even came with its own paintbrush and came to stand next to her. In that moment, there was something extremely compelling about him and the soft way he was looking at her. "Rhea al dente."

An unexpected shiver went over her and she knew it was caused by the hot, seductive curve of his mouth. Ace Krux was a man to be reckoned with.

"If you like that, we have a sample," Grandma said as she brushed past Ace.

She went to the shelf and opened a tester jar, then took a white, plastic spoon and ladled out a bit of chocolate into a small plastic cup.

When Rhea reached for it, she pulled the cup back. "Give me your finger."

Before Rhea could really comply, the old woman took Rhea's finger, dipped it in the chocolate, and held it up for Ace to sample. He didn't hesitate to open his mouth and capture her.

Rhea's stomach fluttered as his warm, sensuous tongue encircled the pad of her fingertip while he held her hand in his to keep it in his mouth. He nipped her flesh ever so gently with his teeth while he stared at her with a hot, needful look. His masculine scent of aftershave and shampoo filled her head, making her heart pound.

Never in her life had she been so unexpectedly turned on by any man. This was intrusive and rude and . . . and she was dying to know what his lips would taste like.

Get a grip!

Rhea pulled her finger out. "I hope you've had a rabies shot lately."

He laughed at that, then dipped his finger into the cup. "Your turn."

"That is so not sanitary."

"Chicken?"

Rhea couldn't believe he was relying on the childhood tactic. Even worse, she couldn't believe it was working. She wasn't about to let Mr. Perfect Agent get away with it.

It was time Mr. Krux learned a lesson.

Taking his hand into hers, she opened his palm and blew her breath across it. She gave him her best "do me, hotshot" stare before she licked the palm of his hand and took the entire length of his finger into her mouth.

Ace ground his teeth to keep from cursing in blissful agony the instant she started tonguing his finger. That woman had a tongue that poets should write about.

At the very least it deserved a major letter to *Penthouse Forum.*

Every hormone in his body fired as his cock hardened to the point of pain. And with every tiny, erotic stroke of her tongue, he hardened even more.

She growled low in her throat before she took a gentle bite of his skin, then pulled back. "Hershey's is better."

Ace was completely dumbstruck. Since all of his blood had drained to the center of his body, there wasn't much left to understand her words. He only knew she'd stepped away from him and that was the last thing he wanted.

In fact, the only thing he wanted right then was to take her into his arms and taste that sweet, sassy mouth. To pin her to the wall behind her and sate the painful ache in his groin that wanted nothing more than to be naked and sweaty with her.

Rhea was a lot more turned on by what she'd done than she wanted to admit. The truth was, Ace had tasted wonderful. And the look on his face as she tasted him was branded into her consciousness. Her breasts were still swollen and heavy from desire.

How could she be attracted to him? Yeah, he looked great, but he was a pest.

Trying to distract herself, she strolled down an aisle with the most incredibly odd vibrators she'd ever seen. Some of them looked like penises and some of them just looked weird. One in particular had two penises pointing away from each other.

Tilting her head to study it, Rhea paused and frowned.

Ace gave a low, amused laugh as he came up behind her. He was so close, she could actually feel the heat from his body. Feel the intensity of his presence. He might as well be touching her for all the damage he was doing to her willpower.

"You really haven't ever been in one of these stores before have you?" he asked her.

She shook her head. "I had no idea that these"—she gestured toward the myriad of battery-operated boyfriends—"came in so many shapes, colors, or textures. Good grief. Do people really use these?"

As his body brushed against her, she could feel his taut erection. He'd been right. He was a large man, and the thought of that electrified her as he reached for one of the illicit packages. "Yeah, they do, at least I know they use them in porn flicks."

She gave him an arched, censoring look.

He actually looked offended. "What? My cousin Vito produces porn films for a small, independent studio. Much to the horror of my grandparents, he talks about it at every Christmas party."

Relieved more than she wanted to admit, she shook her head. "You have the strangest family."

"And you've spent as much time in Beverly Hills as you've spent in adult stores if you believe that. Trust me, where I grew up, my family were the most normal ones on the block."

"And now I know why I've never made it a habit to frequent either place." Rhea folded her arms over her chest. "So what exactly will I need for this . . . excursion?"

Ace returned the "item" in his hand to the shelf. "I vote we ease our way into this. For one thing, no gags, since gagging Bender would defeat the purpose of getting him to talk."

"That makes sense."

Ace headed over two aisles to where they had a display of restraints. "Something simple. Handcuffs."

Rhea studied the variety of manacles they had. An unbidden image of Ace spread out naked on her bed flashed through her mind, and in spite of what she would ever admit, she had to say it was an incredible thought.

*Oh, jeez, don't make him right! He would be flattered to no end
to know that you really are picturing him naked.*

"Some of this stuff looks like it ought to be illegal," she
said, trying to distract herself again.

Ace shrugged. "Personally, I'm not into the rough stuff,
but there are all kinds out there."

"I'm just glad I'm not one of them and that I'm licensed
to carry a concealed weapon should I ever have the misfor-
tune of meeting one in a dark alley."

"Yeah." Ace grabbed two pairs of velvet-lined cuffs. He
held them like a man who truly had no interest in using
them.

"You really aren't into it, are you?" she asked in surprise.
As gung ho and adventurous as he was in everything else,
she would have thought he was a regular porn-meister.

"No. I like my sex the good old-fashioned way. Down
and dirty."

She rolled her eyes at him. "You know, there for a
minute, I was starting to like you."

"Only a minute?"

"You're right. It was more like ten seconds."

"Okay, for that, I vote for this." He picked up a cat-o'-
nine-tails that was made of thick leather straps.

"Fine." She left him and went to the bustier rack, where
she quickly found a frilly red number made out of satin and
feathers. "What do you think of this?"

He grinned. "I like it."

"Good. What size are you?"

"Pardon?"

Grandma laughed. "I have his size in back."

"No!" Ace snapped. "I only have one rule in life: no drag."

"Why not?" Rhea teased. "You allergic to satin?"

"No, but this"—he picked up the thong part of it—"would give me a wedgie from hell. No, thank you."

She tsked at him, then put it back.

Ace stopped as they passed a tall, thin silver canister that held several long feathers. His look turned speculative, then wicked. "Tickle your ass with a feather?"

"Excuse me?"

He cleared his throat. "I said, particularly nice weather?"

Rhea screwed her face up. "Oh, please, don't tell me you're a fan of *Up the Academy?*"

Ace was stunned that Rhea knew his vague reference to the offbeat, early-eighties film. "So how many times have *you* watched it?"

"More than I cared to. It was my older bother's favorite movie in high school, and I curse the day they ever turned it into a videotape."

Ace laughed, amazed at just how much he enjoyed their verbal sparring and her unique views of the world. "Hey, I defend your brother's taste in movies."

"You would." But the dancing light in her eyes said that she wasn't as offended as she pretended.

Better still, she picked up one of the feathers and added it to the cuffs.

"You gonna let me?" he asked hopefully.

"Oh, no, you're the slave, remember? You have to do what I say."

"Yeah, but don't slaves get rewards?"

"No." She sashayed past him.

Maybe slaves didn't get rewarded, but before they finished this detail, Ace fully intended to. He'd been too hot for this women far too long to not at least get a small taste of that wisecracking mouth.

As for the rest of her . . .

Ace wasn't the kind of man to let something he wanted get away from him, and he wasn't about to let Rhea tie him down without both of them getting a taste of something decadent.

CHAPTER TWO

*R*hea kept glancing up from under her eyelashes while she ate. Ace seemed incredibly
focused on her.

Too focused. She was beginning to feel like a piece of
prey under the hungry stare of a powerful lion. Little did he
know that this bunny, much like the one in *Monty Python
and the Holy Grail,* had sharp, vicious teeth.

She sipped her wine. "If you're trying to make me nervous, Ace, you can hang it up. I don't scare easily."

He arched a brow at her comment as he continued to
watch her. "I'm not trying to make you nervous, Rhea, I'm
only trying to figure you out. You're normally so cool at
work that I find it amazing how much you're not when
you're out of the Bat Tower." The Bat Tower was the pet
name of the BellSouth building in downtown Nashville
where the BAD offices were hidden under the guise of a
BellSouth department door in a secured area of the building
that no one but their people could access.

Rhea set her glass aside and answered snidely, "It's all the chemicals in the air there. They solidify my blood cells until I'm nothing but a statue."

His warm laughter washed over her. Ace was a lot easier to talk to than she would have thought. Her first impression of him when they'd met three years ago had been less than flattering.

Okay, she'd hated him.

He'd shown up to work in a pair of ragged jeans with a T-shirt and a flippant attitude that had set off her ire immediately. She took her job seriously, while Ace took few things seriously—or at least it had seemed like that in the beginning.

It wasn't until she'd seen him in action that she'd developed some respect for his abilities and learned that he really did take his job with the same grave responsibility as the rest of them.

Since he came from a Hollywood family, he was a consummate actor. But that too left her wondering what the real Ace Krux was like. How much of even this charming man eating with her was real and how much of it was an act?

He paused while cutting his steak and looked at her. "Why do I have the sudden feeling that I'm some lab experiment gone wrong and you're the scientist trying to figure out why?"

"You're perceptive. Not about being an experiment. I was just wondering how a guy like you ends up working for the government."

He wiped his mouth before taking a drink of his beer. "In a nutshell, Joe."

That wasn't what she was expecting to hear. "Joe?"

"Yeah. We went to college together out in California. I didn't know what I wanted to do with my life, other than anything that didn't have Hollywood in it. I didn't even know what to major in. When I started my second year, Joe was my roommate, and even though he was only nineteen, he knew exactly what he wanted. While the rest of us went out drinking and partying all the time, he stayed in the room studying."

"That sounds like Joe to me."

"Yeah. One night, I actually got him totally bombed out of his mind and found out a lot about him. He wasn't there for an education, he was there because he wanted to make a difference. He wanted his life to matter to people and he could care less if he made any money so long as he could help the people who needed it. He was the most driven human being I'd ever met, and it was the first time in my life that I ever really respected anyone."

Rhea agreed. Joe was a hard man not to respect. "I still can't understand why a guy like you wanted to save the world. You just don't strike me as an altruist."

He snorted at that. "You want to know the real truth of why I'm here?"

She nodded.

"While we were roommates, I found out that Joe had never been to DC before and that one of the things he wanted most was to see the Smithsonian before he died. It was the same year that they were doing the *Star Trek* exhibit, which I thought would be cool to see since one of the costumes they had on display was one my mother had worn when she played some alien princess out to seduce Kirk."

In spite of herself, she was intrigued that she had probably seen that episode a dozen times in her life without ever guessing that one of the women after Kirk would have a son who would one day end up working with her. "Your mother was in a *Star Trek* episode?"

"Oh, yeah. She made tons of appearances in shows and movies before she married my dad and started having us."

Rhea hated to admit it, but she was fascinated by Ace's past. He'd had quite a childhood out in Hollywood. "Given that, I can see why you wanted to go, but it was really nice of you to take Joe along."

"Yeah, well, like I said, I admired him and it wouldn't have been half as much fun alone. So the two of us were there in the Smith along with several hundred other people, including families with small children and babies in strollers, when this voice came over the intercom telling us that there was a bomb threat and that the entire building had to be evacuated immediately."

Rhea saw red at that. It was just that kind of needless panic and fear that she hated.

"I don't think I've ever been more scared in my life," Ace confessed.

"*You* were scared and you admit it?"

He shrugged. "Hard to believe, but, yeah, as we filed down the halls and then single file down some metal back stairs, I really did expect a bomb to go off and kill us all. I kept looking around at all the faces of the people who had innocently gone there that day for no other reason than to see a little bit of our history, and I thought, what kind of dick would blow up the Smith? I mean, I knew such things happened, but it was the first time it was personal.

"And as we stood out in the Mall, waiting for the bomb squad to search the building, I got really angry as I looked around at all the different buildings that make up the Smith and thought about the irreplaceable items each one held. All the pieces of history that could have been lost to future generations . . . *The Spirit of St. Louis,* the Hope diamond, the original 'Star-Spangled Banner,' hell, even my mother's costume and the Lone Ranger's mask. But worse than that were all the children who were around me who would have been history themselves. It wasn't right, and for the first time, I really understood what motivated Joe to right the wrongs of the world. So I decided I wanted to do something with my life too. After graduation, we packed our things, moved to DC, and started applying for jobs. Within six months, he ended up in the CIA while I joined the SS."

She was impressed at the timetable and their impetus, especially for Ace. "That must have been scary for you guys to head out across the country on your own."

He shrugged. "Not really. When you have the kind of money and connections my family does, there's not a lot of risk in much of anything. My dad bought me a Georgetown brownstone for graduation, so it was just a matter of finding our places in the world."

"Wow," she said sarcastically, remembering how many times in her childhood they had barely made ends meet. "It must be nice to chomp the silver spoon and know that no matter what you do, you have a safety net."

He seemed to ignore her sarcasm. "Sometimes, but if you're not careful, that safety net can quickly turn into a noose to hang you."

His perception stunned her. Ace had real depth . . . that really was the last thing she'd expected from him, and it made him all the more alluring to her. "How do you mean?"

"I've seen a lot of my friends and family end up on drugs and totally screwed up emotionally because they have no concept of how hard life is for those who lack. To them a crisis is that the detail place didn't deliver the Ferrari in time for the party and now they have to take the Bentley instead. God forbid."

She watched the way the candlelight played in his dark blond hair while he ate some of his steak. The light danced on the sharp angles of his cheeks and jaw, making her wonder what it would feel like to trace that strong jawline with her finger. She shivered with the thought of it. It had really been far too long since she'd been with a man. Even longer since she'd last felt this insane need to reach out and touch one.

Why she would feel that with Ace, she couldn't imagine. Though to be honest, he was starting to grow on her now that he was talking to her and not sniping at her.

"How is it you escaped that fate?" she asked, more interested in the answer than she should have been.

"Again, I have to say Joe. He was the first poor person I'd

ever really gotten to know. Here I was stressing out over whether I should go to Cancún or Rio for spring break while he was sneaking fruit into his backpack so that he'd have something to eat over the weekend rather than starve. I shudder to think what I might have become had I not lucked out when they were handing out roommate assignments."

Rhea thought about that in silence while Ace continued to eat. He really was beginning to intrigue her with his stories.

And that terrified her.

Even so, she wanted to know more about him. "So how did you end up with the name Thaddeus?" she asked, changing the subject. "That just doesn't seem to fit you at all."

He groaned as if the name pained him greatly. "Before my dad was a director, he was a stunt double. My mother thought it would be funny to name all of us after whatever character he was playing when we were conceived."

"Really? How fun." But for her life, she couldn't think of a single movie from the time of their birth with a character by that name. "So who was Thaddeus?"

He took another drink of beer. "It's an old TV western from 1971. *Alias Smith and Jones.* Ben Murphy played Jed "Kid" Curry, aka Thaddeus Jones, and hence my name. I suppose it could be worse. Had Dad been dark-haired, I'd have been named Hannibal after the Pete Deul character."

She cringed for him. "Lucky you, indeed. So where did you get the nickname Ace?"

"John Wayne."

She rolled her eyes. "I was being serious."

"I *am* serious. He was a longtime friend of my grandfather's. One night, about a year before he died, he was at my grandfather's house playing cowboy with me. I wanted a cool outlaw name, so the Duke dubbed me Ace Hijinx, Kid Outlaw."

A rush of warmth went through her. How sweet.

But Ace's face turned deeply sad. "I was only eight when he died, and when my mother came in to tell me he was gone, I told her I would never use another name again. The Duke had named me Ace, and Ace I would be."

Her heart ached for him and the pain she saw on his face. "You loved him."

"Yeah. He was like another grandfather to me." Ace returned to his meal.

Rhea sat quietly as she thought over all of the stories and things he'd told her tonight. "You must have had a fascinating life, knowing all those celebrities."

He took it with an uncharacteristic dose of humility. "Yes and no. At the end of the day, fame is fleeting, and it really is true, we all get dressed the same way every day. The only difference between someone who works at McDonald's and a Hollywood diva is the size of the paycheck and ego. I've seen fame destroy far more lives than it's built."

Yes, there was a lot more to Ace than she would have given credit.

He met her gaze, and the intensity of those blue eyes made her shivery. "I have a lot more respect for someone like Joe, who had every mark against him and yet he fought his way out of poverty, turned his life around, and made something out of himself, than I do for all the rich kids who take their trust funds and party in the Caymans. Trust me, I'd much rather hang out with the Joes of the world."

He took another bite of his steak. "So what about you? Where did you grow up?"

Rhea sighed wistfully as she remembered her small hometown. "Starkville, Mississippi. The biggest celebrity I ever met growing up was the man in Tupelo who sold Elvis his first guitar."

Ace smiled at that as if Mr. Hollywood really was impressed.

"I hope you gave that man a big thank-you."

She didn't respond.

"So what about your parents?" he asked. "You never really talk about them."

Rhea's heart wrenched as she thought about her mother and father. "No, I don't."

Uncomfortable with the turn in conversation, she cleared her throat. "So tell me about Bender."

"Let's go back to the parent thing. I've spilled my guts to you, the least you could do is tell me something about *your* parents." Ace watched as her brown eyes actually teared up. "Rhea?"

"There's nothing to tell."

He didn't need his instincts to tell him she was hiding something. It was painfully obvious.

Before he could ask her anything else, she excused herself and headed for the restroom. Ace got up to follow her.

"What are you doing?" she asked as he pulled her to a stop in the lobby. "You're not planning on following me into the ladies' room, are you?"

"No. I just want to know why the thought of your parents upsets you so much. Most people don't get teary-eyed when they think of them."

Rhea covered her lips with her hand as she struggled with the pain that still ached raw and deep inside her soul. She always got emotional when she thought of her parents. How could she not?

It was something she struggled with every day, and not even the passage of time could take away the sting of it. That was the bad thing about senseless violence. It left a haunting mark on the lives it scarred.

She didn't want to talk about it and yet she found herself confiding in him for some reason she couldn't even begin to understand. "Do you remember Pan Am flight 103?"

"The Lockerbie, Scotland, bombing?"

"Yeah," she said, forcing herself not to get emotional. But it was hard. "My parents were on that flight, coming home for Christmas from a business trip. My grandmother, brother, sister, and I were putting up the Christmas tree, listening to the news and talking about what we'd do when they got home, when we heard about it."

She choked as she saw that day again clearly in her mind. "My grandmother had been about to put the glass angel on top of the tree when they announced it. It was a special edition Lenox ornament that she had guarded all my life. She dropped it to the floor, where it shattered like our hearts. My sister started screaming and I just stood there in complete shock as I stared at the broken glass on the floor, unable to move or breathe. My grandmother was so upset by the news that she ended up having a stroke later that night."

Ace could see the agony plainly on Rhea's face and it made his own chest tight.

The look she gave him tore through him. "Do you know what the human soul sounds like when it screams in utter agony? It echoes through your body until you're sure it will shatter your eardrums. Only no one else can hear it. Only you do. One minute, I was just a kid, dreaming about picking out a prom dress with my mother, having my dad teach me to drive that summer, and in the next everything about my life was irrevocably changed.

"I no longer had parents to be there when I graduated, to nag me to get married before I turned thirty. No Mom for the mother-daughter tea at my sorority or Dad to help me lug boxes into my dorm room. And all because of a senseless act of violence. It is harsh and it hurts and no child should ever feel like I did in that moment. No one should ever lose a loved one like that. No one."

He didn't know how she held herself so composed. Nothing but absolute anguish was in her eyes.

"Two hundred and fifty-nine families were shattered that day, and I want to make sure that no one will *ever* feel the pain that went through me when I realized my mom and dad weren't coming home ever again. So that, Mr.

Krux, is why when you say the word *terrorist,* I get pissed."

"And you have every right to. I'm sorry, Rhea. I really am."

She nodded. "I know. Now if you'll excuse me, I really need to go to the bathroom for a minute."

Ace stood back and watched as she headed toward the door. She walked slowly and methodically, but he had a good idea she was going in there so that she could fall apart.

Damn. He shouldn't have pushed. But how could he have guessed that? His stupid story at the Smith was paltry compared to hers. And people like her were why his job meant so much to him. It was what kept him going on no sleep, and why he never wanted to get serious with a woman.

His job was stressful enough, the last thing he needed was a woman who wanted time from him that he couldn't give her.

Sighing, he went back to the table to wait for Rhea to return.

When she came back a few minutes later, he could tell she'd been crying. Her features were pinched, her eyes only a little red, but it was enough to let him know what she'd done in the bathroom.

"You are without a doubt the strongest woman I have ever met," he said, toasting her with his beer. "I really admire you, Rhea."

Rhea frowned at him as she reached for her wine and clinked it lightly against his beer bottle. "Now I'm really suspicious of you, Ace. What do you have up that sleeve of yours?"

"Nothing but bare flesh, which you will see all for your-self tomorrow morning." He winked at her, which caused her to get that familiar angry spark in her brown eyes.

Now that was much better than her sadness. If he kept her angry, she wouldn't be able to focus on anything else.

"You know, I've always read about incorrigible men, but you really are, aren't you?"

He laughed at that. "Beat me with all your whips and quips, baby."

She gave him a half-teasing, half-sinister smile. "I plan to."

"That's all right. It'll be worth it so long as you kiss all my boo-boos afterward."

"Oh, you are a quick one, Mr. Krux."

"But the real question is, am I charming you out of your pants?" He wagged his eyebrows at her.

"You're working on it, aren't you?"

"I'm trying to."

She gave him a heated once-over. "You might stand more of a chance if I didn't know how many other women you've already charmed out of *their* pants and then danced right out of their lives."

He held his hands up in mock surrender. "Those are all lies. I was framed."

"Yeah, right."

And yet she was beguiled by him and that infectious debonair attitude of his. He really was starting to charm her out of her pants, and that scared her more than the thought of dominatrix training.

She really did want him. How could she not? He had been strangely understanding about her parents, and now she realized he was trying to distract her to get her mind off it.

Ace really did have a heart and a soul underneath that trying facade.

"So let's do some business," she said as she returned to her grilled chicken. "Tell me all about Bender."

"He's a total freak. Just your kind of guy."

She laughed. "Sounds more like your type. Maybe I should have gotten you that bustier after all."

"Stop with the bustier jokes." He shuddered. "Every time you talk about it, I get this image in my head that has scarred me for life."

"What image?"

"My aunt was one of the women who did the makeup for *Tootsie*. To get ready for it, she practiced on my dad. I came home from school to find him decked out in the complete getup: sequins, wig, earrings, makeup, you name it. Forget horror, that was the scariest thing I've ever seen. My dad made one ugly woman."

Rhea laughed again. "Are you serious?"

"Oh, yeah. You couldn't pay me enough to ever get me near female clothes . . . unless I'm taking them off a female body."

"Ace!" she growled. "Focus on something other than your hormones."

"I would try to focus on your hormones, but you get pissed every time I do."

"We are here to work."

"Yeah, but for once my work entails me getting you naked."

"I am not getting naked for you."

"Nearly naked then."

"Ace . . ."

"Okay, okay, I'll stop and brief you for real."

And for once he held to his word. They finished up dinner while he went over every nuance of the case and every sick fetish he had uncovered about Bender.

The more Rhea learned, the more she became aware of just how important it was to get this man out of commission.

After Ace had paid their check, they walked out to the parking lot and got back into her car, where he was just a little too close to her. It was hard to ignore a man whose presence dominated the small area. The warm scent of his skin filled her head and it was all she could do to focus on traffic and not those teasing lips that she suddenly wanted to taste.

"So how do I find my way to your bed anyway?" Ace asked as she backed out of the space.

Rhea gave him a hooded stare. "You don't have enough charm, wit, or money to ever get into my bed."

His face was a mask of wickedness. "Wait a sec. I'm supposed to be at your place tomorrow so you can tie me to your bed, remember? I can't do that if I don't know where you live."

Oh, yeah. "Well, you are a superspy. You could sic Carlos on me and find out."

He laughed. "Yeah, but Tee has the payroll. She'd be faster."

"True, but lucky for you, I'll make it even easier than that. I live in Franklin, down on Church Street."

"The historic area?"

She nodded. "It's a small 1930s cottage, painted creamy yellow with a burgundy door and black iron fence. You can't miss it."

"Creamy yellow? That's different from regular yellow how?"

"It's lighter, paler."

She could see from the corner of her eye that he had that man face that said, "Women and their weird colors."

They were quiet as she drove him back to the lot where he had his car parked. She pulled up beside his Viper. "See you tomorrow."

The intensity of those eyes on her body made her hot. Feverish. "Yes, you will. *All* of me." He glanced to the bag she'd tossed in the backseat. "Don't forget to lay out our toys."

"I shudder at the thought." But the real problem was that after tonight she didn't truly shudder in revulsion. She shivered in anticipation.

A foreign part of her was actually looking forward to it.

"You shudder, huh?" Ace leaned over, and before she realized what he was doing, he kissed her fiercely.

Her entire body sizzled at the taste of those firm lips

against hers. She opened her mouth to taste him fully and let the scent of warm, spicy cologne and Ace fill her head.

This man really knew how to give a kiss. Forget his gun, his mouth should have been registered as a lethal weapon. His tongue swept against hers in a promising, hungry fashion that left her completely breathless before he pulled back to give her a hot, lustful look. Her entire body was on fire and it was all she could do not to pull him back to her and taste him again.

"That was daring of you," she said, her voice remarkably calm given the havoc of her body. "Especially since you know I'm packing heat."

He laughed. "True, but I thought I should at least kiss you before you see me naked." He opened the car door. "Night, Rhea."

"Night, Ace."

He got out and slammed the door shut, then got into his Viper.

Rhea watched as he buckled himself in. He paused to give her a devilish grin before he squealed out of the parking space and headed for the entrance.

Her body still on fire from the passion of that kiss, she followed him out of the lot at a much more subdued pace even though a part of her was racing even more than he was.

"It's just a kiss."

But it had been a great one.

And tomorrow she really would see him naked . . .

★　　★　　★

Ace pulled his black Viper into Rhea's driveway. He still couldn't believe he was going to do this. He should actually thank Bender for being such a sick bastard since Bender was the one finally giving him a way to get close to Rhea.

God help him, but he'd been in love with her since the first time he'd seen her. And she had shined him on without a second glance.

Unused to having to beg or fight for a woman's attention, Ace had walked away, wishing he knew of something to make her attracted to him. She'd always been so reserved toward him, if not downright nasty. No matter what he tried, it always seemed to be the wrong thing with her.

Until last night.

His lips still sizzled from her kiss. His body burned from the thought of having her tie him up . . .

You're a sick man yourself, Ace.

No, he was a desperate one. There had always been something about Rhea that set his entire body on fire. It was why he'd bribed Hunter to change cubes with him in the office. Hunter had pretended that being under the air vent was messing with his allergies. So Ace had "volunteered" to take his desk.

It had been the best and worst $3,000 he'd ever spent. The best because it forced Rhea to acknowledge him when he was in the office. The worst because being so close to her was complete torture.

Ace pulled off his sunglasses and set them in the passenger seat.

It was the moment of truth.

Getting out, he slammed the door shut and sauntered up the driveway when what he really wanted to do was sprint. But the last thing he wanted was for Rhea to know just how badly he wanted her.

No, coolness would win this. Or if not, it would at least save his dignity.

Rhea saw Ace leave his car and saunter with that masculine, predatory lope toward her front door. He looked totally edible as he came closer to her lair.

Yes, he was sexy. Yes, he was hot, but she wasn't about to play into that overinflated ego of his. She had to be cool and dispassionate about wanting to take a bite out of that man. She should never have spent time with him last night. Somehow, he'd actually become human to her and not a total scumbag. A tiny part of her was even starting not only to like him, but respect him as well.

He knocked on her door.

Rhea clenched and unclenched her fists, then shook them in an effort to calm down. She had to get a grip on herself. Quick.

Taking a deep breath, she opened the door to find Ace standing there with one hip cocked and a seductive smile on his face.

"Morning, sunshine," he said.

"Morning." Rhea stepped back to let him enter.

He gave her that wicked, charming smile. "Now this is where in Hollywood they would cue 'Bad to the Bone' to play as I entered your house."

Rhea rolled her eyes. "Oh, please! Ace, you're so bad."

"To the bone, baby," he sang.

"Stop that!"

He didn't, instead, he broke into a perfect rendition of George Thorogood. The man really did have a great voice.

Rhea closed her door. "All right, I get it."

He didn't stop; worse, he literally pinned her to the door and held her trapped between the wood and his long, lush body. He lowered his tone so that he could sing in her ear without causing her pain. His voice was low and sultry and it reverberated though her.

The pain came not from his body pressing against hers or her voice ringing in her ears, it came from the deep-seated ache at the core of her body that throbbed with a piercing need for *him*.

"I want to be yours, pretty baby, yours and yours alone."

That sounded too good to be true and she knew that things that seemed to be too good, always were.

"Should I get my saxophone?" she asked, trying to get her thoughts on something other than him being naked in her arms.

That succeeded in breaking his song. "You got one?"

"Yeah, I do."

"Cool. Can you play?"

He still hadn't moved back and she couldn't move away without brushing even more of her body up against his.

If she did that, she'd be lost, as badly as she wanted him. There was no way she could feel all that hard, lean muscle and not kiss him again.

Or do something she might later regret.

She cleared her throat before she answered his question. "Not well, but I can hammer out a few notes now and again that don't make the neighborhood dogs bark."

He laughed as he lifted up one hand to play with a stray black curl of her hair. She had to force herself not to lean her head forward the few inches it would take to bury her nose in the hollow of his throat and just inhale his spiced, manly scent.

Or better yet, lick that tawny skin that covered the hot tendon in his neck. . . .

"In that case, I need to introduce you to my little brother, Aramis. He used to torture his guitar to the point I sold it for a dollar to our gardener."

"You did not!"

"Yeah, I did. Still have my father's handprint on my butt to prove it. Want to see?"

Rhea snorted at him even though the offer was extremely tempting. "Why does everything have to get back to me seeing you naked?"

He smiled at her. "Ulterior motives."

The worst part was that Rhea really did want to see what he kept hidden under those clothes. She'd spent many hours last night after their kiss wondering how much of his ego was boasting and how much was true.

He dipped his head down to nuzzle her cheek.

For a full second, she couldn't move as she savored the feel of him there. But somewhere in the back of her mind, warning bells went off.

"Would you like some coffee or juice?" she asked, pushing him away before she headed toward her kitchen. Yowza, but he had a hard body. Just the brief contact of her hand on his chest was enough to let her know he was built of solid muscle.

Disappointment flashed across his face, only to be quickly replaced by a grim determination. "Juice would be great." He followed after her and took a seat at her breakfast counter while she went to her fridge.

She could feel his gaze on her body. Turning her head, she saw confirmation. He was staring at her butt as if he were caressing her in his mind. Her entire body burned.

Rhea almost dropped the juice. Tightening her grip, she pretended to ignore him and went to get a glass. "So your brother is named Aramis, huh? Your dad must have been in *The Three Musketeers.*"

"Yes, and Aramis is grateful every day of his life that Dad didn't double for Christopher Lee."

"Why?"

"He played Rochefort."

She laughed as she poured the juice. "Yeah, I can see where that might be bad. But had your father doubled for Michael York, Aramis would be D'Artagnan. That could have been cool." She handed him his juice.

"Maybe," Ace said before he took a sip. "But no one would ever be able to spell it."

The doorbell rang.

Grateful for the interruption, Rhea put the juice back in the fridge. "That must be our instructor."

She headed back to the door, unsure of what to expect. The woman's name was Beullah Mueller, and for some reason she pictured an extremely rigid German woman who looked like the gym teacher from the movie *Porky's*, complete with hair rolled into sausages around her head.

The reality was worse.

"Hi," the woman said, not in a German-accented voice, but in a normal American one.

"Beullah?" Rhea asked, unsure if this was the right woman.

Surely not.

Around the age of forty-five, the woman in front of her was of average height, slender, and was dressed in pink designer sweats. She had a large, navy blue gym bag slung over her shoulder. Something about her reminded Rhea of Meredith Baxter-Birney from *Family Ties*.

She looked wholesome and sweet.

Beullah smiled warmly. "I know. I look like someone's middle-aged mother and not a dominatrix instructor. But in my day . . . I have to tell you, I have whipped many a man's ass and enjoyed it thoroughly."

There was something extremely incongruous about that coming out of the mouth of a woman who looked as if she ought to be in a peanut butter commercial.

"Okay," Rhea said, stepping back to let the woman in. "I don't suppose I want to ask how it is Tee knew to call you, do I?"

"We go to the same spa and health club. I have to tell you that Tee is something else. She bends like a pretzel."

"Oh, jeez, now there's an image I want burned out of my memory. I'll never be able to look Tee in the eye again," Ace said as he joined them.

Beullah smiled. "You must be Ace. Tee told me to give you an extra hard time."

"I'm sure she did, just as I'm sure you will."

Rhea had to admit she didn't like the way Beullah was looking at Ace, like a starving woman staring at a steak.

Beullah waltzed into the living room and placed her bag on the coffee table. "Tee said she liked the two of you a lot and that you were ready to get more adventurous in your relationship, so here I am."

"Pardon?" Rhea asked.

Beullah waved her hand. "Oh, don't be bashful. I've worked with lots of couples who have gotten bored with the missionary position and are looking for new ways to spice up their sex. I had this couple once who started out normal as pie, and the next thing I knew, they had more body piercings than Marilyn Manson and Christina Aguilera combined. He really liked feeling the cat-o'-nine-tails whip across his pe—"

"TMI," Ace said quickly, cutting her off. "Way too much information for me."

Rhea agreed completely, but couldn't resist teasing him. "I don't know, Ace. That sounds like fun. Sure you don't want to give it a try?"

"Nothing painful comes near the area," he said, indicating his entire groin. "Nothing."

"Now, now," Beullah said as she unzipped her bag. "You

two have to learn to trust each other. That's rule number one about being a couple. If you're to have a healthy relationship, you have to learn to express your needs and fears to each other without dread or inhibition."

So that was the story Tee was using for this. Rhea and Ace were supposed to be a couple wanting to add spice to their sex life. Nice lie. Tee could have filled them in on it first.

"Well," Rhea said wistfully, "you know how it goes. Even the hottest piece of cheese eventually goes bad. I never thought I'd get bored with Ace, but look at him . . . My cheddar turned into Gouda on me."

"Hey, I resent that." Ace's tone was offended. "I'm not the prude here. You're the one who walks around in shirts buttoned all the way up to your nose and pants or long skirts. You know it wouldn't hurt you to wear a miniskirt and low-cut blouse once in a while."

Rhea arched her brow at that. Ace had been paying attention to her clothes. Who knew?

"Now, now," Beullah said in a voice that held the full authority of a woman used to being in charge. "There's no need in blaming each other. Two days with me and you two will know all there is to know about how to make each other beg for your attention."

She opened her bag wider and searched through plastic bags. "You," she said to Ace. "Take off your clothes."

He went completely stiff. "Bullshit."

Beullah pulled out a whip. "Take off your clothes, slave. Now."

"No."

She snapped the whip at Ace, who caught it without flinching when it wrapped itself around his forearm. "Whips don't do it for me, baby. I'm not a lion and you're not going to tame me like one." He jerked the whip out of her hands.

Beullah looked at him with a newfound respect. She glanced over to Rhea. "You certainly have your hands full, huh?"

"You've no idea."

Beullah retrieved her whip.

"C'mon, Ace," Rhea said. "Time to play."

He growled low in his throat before he started unbuttoning his shirt.

Beullah smiled approvingly. "That's it, Rhea. You have to take charge of your slave and show him who's boss." Beullah unzipped her sweatshirt top.

Rhea's eyes bulged as she realized that beneath that average outfit, Beullah wore a leather corset that had studded metal cups that covered her breasts.

Beullah acted as if there were nothing unusual about her state of dress. "First thing you have to do, Rhea, is get used to your role as mistress. You need to be completely comfortable in this."

Beullah pulled her pants off. She wore a pair of black fishnets that were held up by bloodred ribbons. The back of the corset was a thong that left more of Beullah exposed than Rhea had ever wanted to see.

Rhea could feel herself gaping. "I could *never* feel comfortable in *that.*"

"Sure you could," Beullah and Ace said at once.

"No, really," Rhea insisted. "How about a T-shirt and . . ." Her voice trailed off as Beullah pulled out three small plastic baggies.

"This should fit. Tee gave me your size and told me to pick out something extra rough."

Beullah opened one bag and handed Rhea two pieces of something she would have sworn was an arm sling . . . for a very small child.

"Don't be bashful," Beullah said. "I'm sure Ace has seen you naked enough not to care, and you haven't got anything I don't." She looked at her speculatively. "At least I hope you don't, and even if you do, I'm sure I've seen it on someone else."

Yeah . . . Little did Beullah know Ace had never seen her undressed in either of their lives. But then Bender would have the same problem. She was going to have to wear this for not only a complete stranger, but a demented one at that.

Okay, Rhea, you can do this.

No, I can't.

Yes, you can. Do it.

Determined to go through with this, she started for her bedroom. At times she really, truly hated her job, and now she knew why she'd given up fieldwork to begin with.

It sucked.

"And don't forget this." Beullah handed her another red-tinted plastic bag and a smaller bag.

Rhea was too scared to even look at what it contained. Ignoring Ace, who watched her with a hot, intense stare, she crept to her room down the hallway, where she would hopefully find her courage lurking someplace.

By the time she was dressed in the tiny, shiny PVC halter top and thong bottom, Rhea had almost convinced herself that this wasn't so bad. After all, women wore less than this on beaches in Rio.

Not that much less, but somewhat less.

Of course it would help if the bottom wasn't crawling into places the good Lord never meant neoprene to touch. Rhea opened the bags to find a pair of fishnet stockings and six-inch-spike-heeled PVC boots. Oh, yeah, these looked lethal.

And poor Ace thought his padded handcuffs would be used.

"How long have you two been dating?" Beullah asked while Ace waited without his shirt on for Rhea to return.

He kept his arms folded over his chest, wondering what Rhea would look like when she came back.

"Three years," he said to Beullah's question. The first rule of lying was to stick close to the truth. Since he'd known Rhea that long, it seemed a safe guess.

"Do you love her?"

Rule number two, answer question with question and let the other person draw their own conclusions. "What's not to love?"

Beullah went to her bag and pulled out a pair of tiny leather briefs. "You know, this is what *you're* supposed to wear."

He curled his lip at the thought of that little thing strapped onto him. "I'd rather keep my pants on, thank you."

She clucked her tongue at him. "Aren't you more sexually adventurous than that?"

If it were only a sexual relationship, the answer would be hell no. Unfortunately, more than a relationship was at stake here. If Rhea didn't at least act as if she knew what she was doing, she'd end up killed, and since he was the one who had gotten her into this . . .

Expelling a disgusted breath, he grabbed the briefs from Beullah and realized *brief* was definitely the key word. He might as well be covering a watermelon with a Band-Aid.

Okay, maybe that was an exaggeration, but that's what it felt like.

Ace headed for the open door in the hallway that led to Rhea's bathroom. Ignoring the feminine pink-and-white-flowered decor, he closed the door, then pulled his shoes, socks, and pants off.

Just as he reached for his briefs, the door opened.

Rhea froze at the unexpected sight of Ace completely naked in her bathroom. Her heart hammering, all she could do was gape.

Hello. He was glorious!

It wasn't as if she hadn't known he'd have a great body. She did. But this . . .

This was heaven. He was so toned, she could see every tendon of muscle. His skin was deep tawny and inviting. Warm and delectable.

He made her mouth water.

And as she stared at him, she realized he was growing hard even before her eyes.

He cursed an instant before he grabbed a pink towel off her counter and covered himself. "Did you need something, Rhea?"

"Damned if I remember what it was now," she confessed. "I have to say, seeing you naked has totally reviled me to utter stupefaction."

He scoffed at that. "Yeah, well, I have to say, I'm enjoying the view myself."

It was time to teach this man a lesson. Rhea narrowed her eyes on him two seconds before she stepped forward and grabbed the towel he was holding. Before she could stop herself, she jerked it free.

"Hey!" Ace snapped as she danced away with it.

Laughing, she ran out of the bathroom with Ace in hot pursuit. They both skidded to a halt as they entered the living room and saw Beullah looking intimidating in her role as mistress.

Rhea didn't protest Ace's taking the towel back and wrapping it quickly around his hips.

"I'll get you later for that," he whispered before he vanished back into the bathroom.

"Good, good, good," Beullah said. "You should play with your slave. Torment him until he knows who the boss is."

Yeah, but in this relationship, Rhea wasn't sure she was any more his boss than he was hers. It seemed to be a mutual game of one-upmanship.

Beullah handed her a cat-o'-nine-tails that was made out of velvet and feathers. It looked more like a cat toy than something designed for sexual stimulation.

Ace returned with the towel wrapped around his hips.

Beullah frowned at him. "Did the briefs not fit?"

"Not in my opinion."

Before either of them could move, Beullah whipped the towel free of his hips to expose the leather briefs.

Rhea burst out laughing.

"Hey!" Ace snapped. "Galaxina, I didn't laugh at you."

"I'm so sorry. That just doesn't look right." And it didn't. Something was profoundly wrong with a man as tough as Ace Krux wearing what amounted to a leather Speedo.

"Who is Galaxina?" Beullah asked.

Rhea struggled to subdue her laughter. "A very cheesy sci-fi movie with Dorothy Stratten."

Beullah humphed, then dropped the towel. "Now we need to set a few ground rules. One, there should always be a safe word that the slave uses to let the master or mistress know when he or she has had enough. I think today we will use Pinocchio."

Amusement flashed across Ace's face. "Pinocchio? The boy made of . . . *wood?*"

Rhea rolled her eyes at him.

Beullah gave him a censoring glare. "You have something against Pinocchio, slave?"

"Well, no." He gave Rhea a playful look. "I just think it's an interesting choice."

"Okay, then," Beullah continued. "Just say Pinocchio to

let Rhea know when she's hit you too hard. Remember, this is for fun and for arousal. The point of this isn't to actually hurt each other."

"Thank you, Lord," Ace said in a relieved tone. "Can I start this whole thing by saying Pinocchio now so that I can get dressed again?"

Rhea rolled her eyes at him.

Beullah looked around the living room. "Now Mistress Rhea, where should we tie up your slave?"

Rhea grinned wickedly with a thought. "The front yard for the neighbors to see?"

"Like hell."

Beullah laughed. "You two certainly have the relationship, don't you? All right, children. We'll start simple. The bedroom."

Ace didn't miss a beat. "Pinocchio."

Rhea put her hands on her hips. "Ace, c'mon, play nice."

Unready to face the Hun with the whip, Ace crossed his arms over his chest and followed Beullah and Rhea to the bedroom in back. He paused in the doorway as he took in the white and pink perfection of Rhea's domain. It was innately feminine.

Better still it was innately Rhea, right down to the soft, sweet scent of her perfume that hovered in the air.

His body stirred instantly and it was all he could do not to close his eyes and just inhale the seductive scent.

"We bought these last night." Rhea handed Beullah the bag full of their toys.

Beullah scoffed at them, "Those are for amateurs."

Ace scoffed back, "Consider me an amateur."

As he reached for the velvet-lined handcuffs, Beullah pulled them away. "You are a very bad slave." She handed the whip to Rhea. "Punish him."

Rhea burst out laughing. "I don't think I can do this. I really don't. I'm just not dominatrix material."

"You have to get into the mind-set. Close your eyes."

Rhea looked at Ace. "Cover me if she makes a weird move?"

"You got it."

Rhea closed her eyes as Beullah came up behind her. "Now picture yourself as the ultimate goddess. You have to embrace your inner womanhood and know that you rule the world."

Rhea could see herself as empress of the universe.

"Imagine men lining up to do your every bidding. You have the power to make them want you. To need you. To do anything to get your approval."

A woman could cozy up to that idea.

"Now open your eyes."

She did and Beullah handed her the whip.

"Now make him serve you!"

Rhea stiffened her spine. "Get on your knees, Ace."

"Pinocchio."

"There is no Pinocchio for you!" Rhea cracked the whip, which would have been more effective had it been made of something other than velvet and feathers.

Ace felt completely ridiculous as he did what she ordered. But then she had to get used to this. Her life would depend on her being able to convince Bender that she was a domi-natrix.

What was a little damaged ego if it saved her life?

"Now grab his hair and pull his head back."

Rhea complied.

Ace stared up at her dark, sinister glare.

It lasted about three seconds before she burst out laughing. She rubbed his head where her hand had been gripping his hair. "I didn't hurt you, did I?"

"No," he said honestly.

"Dominate him, Rhea!"

The problem was Rhea didn't want to dominate him. In truth, she wanted to kiss him as she stared at him looking up at her. She knew this had to be humiliating for him and yet he was going along with it.

For her.

"It's okay, Rhea," he said charitably. "Think of all the times I've pissed you off and you wanted to choke the life out of me."

Strange, as he knelt there, she couldn't think of a single instance. More as if they were all an amalgam, but no one incident stood out as being all that heinous.

"This isn't about violence," Beullah said as she watched them. "It's about trust. You don't want to hurt him, Rhea, you want to pleasure him. You have to learn what his pressure points are and learn to pull back just before you really do hurt him." Beullah took the whip and showed her how to wield it.

Rhea practiced for a few minutes until she got the wrist

action down that would enable her to slap the velvet and feathers against him until they made a popping sound.

"Now make him crawl into the bed."

Yeah, right.

"Jump up, Baby Judy, jump up," Rhea said, using the reference from her favorite Hawaiian Pups song. "Get on the bed."

But as Ace climbed up her comforter, all she could focus on was the glorious sight of his lean, hard body. She watched the muscles working in his back and legs as he positioned himself on her bed.

Yeah, now that was something a woman had dreams about.

"Let your fantasies go wild," Beullah whispered in her ear.

The only problem was, Rhea doubted seriously that the chubby arm's dealer would ever look that good in leather Speedos.

Ace, on the other hand . . .

That butt begged for a nip. All too well she could imagine peeling that leather abomination off that delectable flesh with her teeth. Exploring every inch of the man that it concealed with her fingers . . .

Her mouth.

Beullah handed her a pair of leather manacles. "Now tie him up."

Rhea approached the bed. "Turn over, slave."

Ace wasn't sure what to think as he obeyed. A foreign part of him found Rhea's commanding tone a bit sexy. The comfortable part of him rebelled at her orders.

Luckily he had enough sense to keep playing.

Rhea grabbed his hand and secured it to her bedpost. Her hair fell against his palm as she buckled him in. She had to have the softest hair he'd ever felt, and instead of that damned whip, he wished she'd climb over him and tease him with a beating from her hair.

She walked to the other side of the bed and buckled his other hand.

Ace tried for a quick grope, only to have Rhea give him a menacing frown before she had him all buckled in and unable to get up.

That was something that made him extremely nervous. "I have a question."

"Slaves don't have questions," Beullah snapped.

"Well, this one does. In case some catastrophic event occurs and you two drop dead, is there any way for me to get out of this on my own?"

Rhea laughed. "No, babe, so you better pray nothing happens to us."

"I can see the tabloid headlines now," he muttered.

Beullah clucked her tongue. "Maybe we should gag him."

Before Rhea could say no, Beullah pulled out this strange contraption with a bright orange ball in the center.

Rhea shook her head at it. "Oh, that just looks cruel."

Beullah swung it back and forth by a leather chord as she studied Ace. "You sure you don't want to try it?"

Ace snorted. "No way that's going into my mouth until I see something legal saying it's been thoroughly sterilized and detoxed."

Rhea agreed with that, not to mention she couldn't get Bender to talk if he was wearing a gag. "I think we'll pass on that."

Her face disappointed, Beullah put it back in her bag. Then over the next two hours, she went about explaining the psychology and toys of dominance to Rhea, whose head felt as if it were going to explode from information overload.

Just before lunch, Beullah decided to call it a day.

"I'll just head on back home," she said to Rhea. "And let the two of you practice in private for a while. It'll take you a little time to get really comfortable. Just remember, baby steps. Tomorrow I'll bring some of the more interesting toys."

"Oh, goody," Ace said sarcastically from the bed. "I can't wait."

Rhea grimaced at him. "Ace, be nice or I will use the gag."

They left him tied to the bed while they went to the living room, where Beullah quick pulled on her sweat suit again. She packed up her "toys," then handed Rhea a business card. "Call me if you have any questions or need anything."

"Thanks."

She left Beullah out, then returned to Ace, who looked less than pleased that she had abandoned him.

"Yo, Rhea. Nice of you to go make chitchat at the door with Eva Braun, but you know I'm kind of tired of being locked to this bed while you've given me the hard-on from hell and nothing else, so either let me up or make Mr. Happy happy."

Rhea licked her lips as she let her gaze wander all over every single inch of that divinely male form. She would never get another shot like this one in her life. All morning she had been staring at his body, examining every inch of it, and now she didn't want to beat him. She wanted to touch him.

And it was time to take exactly what she wanted.

"That's not a very nice way to talk to your mistress, slave," she said, cracking her whip against her boots. "What's the magic word for release?"

"Pinocchio."

"That's right, Pinocchio," she said with a coy smile, "and now it's time to see if you're a real boy."

CHAPTER THREE

*A*ce definitely liked the sound of that. But it seemed way too good to be true.

"Don't be a tease, Rhea. It's just cruel."

She sauntered toward him with a walk what stirred every male hormone in his body. She was truly the one hunger he'd had these last couple of years that he'd never been able to sate.

She dragged the whip across her halter that cupped her breasts to perfection. The ends of it fell into the deep valley, where it caressed her bared flesh and made him wonder what the PVC obscured. His cock jerked with need.

"Who said I was teasing?" she asked.

He watched as she approached his feet. Ace held his breath in sweet expectation of her actions.

C'mon, baby, touch me where it counts . . .

Now that they were alone, he let his mind go wild with what he would love to have her to do him.

She licked her lips suggestively as she raked a hot, hungry look over his body. "Hmm . . ." She crawled onto the bed, between his legs. "Where should I begin?"

"A little due north of your current position," he said, his voice thick and hoarse from her torture.

She arched a brow at him. "A little north, huh?" She inched her hand toward his swollen groin.

It was all Ace could do not to squirm at the thought of her cupping him. He'd never felt so alive, so on edge. So damn needful of a woman's touch.

Her hand came closer. Closer. He held his breath as she hovered directly over his cock.

Just as he was sure she would caress him, she veered her hand off and started tickling him.

Ace cursed in frustration as his body spasmed to get away from her questing hands. He wanted her blood for disappointing him like this.

"Pinocchio!" he shouted, knowing she wouldn't listen to him.

She took no mercy on him whatsoever.

Ace tried to grab her or throw her off, but being spread-eagled on her bed didn't lend itself to doing anything more than bouncing her gently. He was completely at her mercy.

"You're going to pay for this when I get loose."

She paused in her torture. "Am I?"

Her touch turned gentle then as she brushed her hand over his painfully erect nipple. To his amazement, she gently massaged the sensitive tip with her fingernail.

Ace growled as chills spread all over him. He tried to kiss her, but she veered her face away while she continued to stroke his chest.

Rhea knew she had no business touching Ace like this

and yet she couldn't stop herself. She'd wanted him at her mercy ever since he'd kissed her.

Now she had him right where she wanted him.

And he didn't seem to be objecting. It was still surprising to her just how much she had enjoyed their exercises with Beullah. She'd discovered a whole new facet of her personality that she hadn't known existed.

"You know, you've been remarkably good through all this." He'd only complained a few times whenever she'd hit him too hard, but overall, he'd been a really good slave as she learned to wield her whip.

Ace felt his heart hammering as she continued to massage his nipple. He was so hard for her that it was painful. "You in those clothes helped," he said, his voice thick and deep.

"Did it?"

He sucked his breath in sharply as she ran her hand across his chest, to his other nipple.

"Rhea, this really is cruel. You've got me way too excited to just cold-shower it."

"No," she said, her breath falling across his bare skin. "Cruel is having to watch you lying here looking all sexy and choice while knowing I could do anything to you I wanted to and you are powerless to stop me. There really is something very sexy about this."

"And what do you want to do with me?"

She moved her hand lower, toward his swollen cock.

Rhea knew she should let him up. She should stop this madness immediately.

If only it were that easy. But the truth was she'd been way

too attracted to him for too long to just let him leave now. Especially after the morning the two of them had shared.

"Would you let me do what I want to you?" she asked him.

"I'm in no position to stop you."

She smiled at him.

Ace held his breath as she moved toward the small leather briefs. He grabbed the leather straps as every nerve ending in his body fired and danced.

Then she did the most shocking thing of all. She bent her head down and tongued the small zipper that bisected the briefs. The sight of her between his legs made his cock jerk. He was so aroused he was almost afraid of embarrassing himself.

Tensing his body in expectation, he watched as she slowly pulled the zipper down with her teeth. It was the most arousing thing he'd ever experienced.

The most erotic thing he'd ever seen. And it was all he could do not to pull his arms out of their sockets in an effort to free himself long enough to grab her and take her the way he wanted to.

Rhea held her breath as Ace's cock sprang free. She pulled back and used her hand to unzip the briefs all the way around to the back until Ace was completely bare to her.

He was gorgeous there.

She watched him carefully. "Beullah said you needed to learn to trust me."

"I don't trust anyone."

"No?" Rhea didn't know where she got her confidence; maybe it was because they had both been so close to naked all morning that she had gotten a lot more comfortable with him.

Or maybe it was that all she had to do was hear Ace's voice and she was immediately wet for him. Aching.

Whatever caused it, she reached around her and undid her halter top.

Ace hissed at the sight of her bared breasts. Her nipples were hard, just begging for a caress and taste.

Then to his dismay, she leaned over him and wrapped the halter around his eyes.

"What are you doing?"

"Blindfolding you. Now you really are at my mercy."

Ace shook his head, wanting to see her. It didn't do a damn bit of good.

Rhea sat back to survey her naked, blind captive. "It must be nerve-racking for you."

"You have no idea."

She laughed. It was really heady to be able to study him without his intense stare distracting her.

His tawny skin was stretched tight over a well-muscled body. He was a large man, all over. Lying beside him, she touched the tip of his cock with her finger. He was already leaking.

Ace growled as she rubbed the tip of her finger back and forth over him.

"Touch me, Rhea."

She traced the outline of veins all the way down to the

base. She'd always been fascinated by the mat of hair on a man's body. Licking her lips, she ran her fingers through the coarse hair until she cupped him. He arched his back.

"Like that, do you?"

"You have to ask?"

She smiled even wider.

Ace ground his teeth as she explored him with a slow, methodical hand that left him breathless and weak. He still couldn't believe she was doing this. Rhea wasn't the kind of woman to just jump into a man's bed.

She was the kind of woman that a man took home and kept.

"If I'm asleep, don't wake me." He hadn't realized he'd spoken aloud until he heard her response.

"Pardon?"

Her hand stopped its sweet torture.

What the hell? He'd come this far. He might as well be honest with her. "You have no idea how many times I have closed my eyes and tried to imagine what your hands would feel like on my body, Rhea. Your lips on mine."

Rhea gently slid her hand up his cock. "Really?"

"Yes." The word was ragged and it excited her even more than his confession.

She pulled her hand back, then laid her body over his, reveling in the sensation of all that steely masculine flesh under her. He felt good.

Too good.

Her heart hammering, she slowly explored the chiseled outline of his jaw with her tongue. She'd always wanted to taste his jawline. He was one of those men who tended to go a couple of days between shaves. Though she didn't like the look of a beard, she loved the sight of his unkempt whiskers.

He lifted his hips so that the tip of his swollen shaft was pressing against the center of her body. She hissed at the sensation. It was making her even wetter. Hotter.

But she wasn't ready to take him in yet.

Sitting up, she leaned over him and kissed that delectable, taunting mouth of his.

Ace couldn't breathe as her tongue swept against his. Her kiss was fierce, demanding, and it whet his appetites for more.

He could just imagine what she must look like sitting on his stomach as he lay completely naked, tied spread-eagled to the posts of her bed.

"Will you take the blindfold off?"

"If I do that, I might come to my senses and chicken out."

"Forget that then."

She laughed low and seductively. "Tell me what you've dreamed of me doing to you, Ace."

"I'm not sure where to start." He couldn't even begin to catalog all of his fantasies about her.

He felt her sliding off him.

Before he could speak, he felt something soft tickling his hip bone. "What is that?"

"The feather," she said a minute before she swept it over his cock.

Ace groaned in ecstasy.

"Have you ever thought of this?"

"Yes," he confessed. "I've seen you drizzle honey on those biscuits you get whenever Tee brings you lunch from the Cracker Barrel. And I've dreamed of coating your entire body in it and licking it off."

Rhea squirmed at the image in her mind that conjured. "What else?"

"I've dreamed of tasting your . . ." Ace caught himself before he said *tits*. Women didn't like that word. "Breasts. Of you sliding them up and down my chest until you go down on me."

"Hmmm."

She stopped tormenting him with the feather. He was afraid he'd offended her until he felt something soft against his cheek. It was her breast. Pulling against the restraints, he opened his lips and turned so that he could taste her swollen nipple as she held herself for him.

Rhea couldn't believe she was doing this and yet she didn't want to stop. The truth was, she'd spent far too many days dreaming of him too. It was why she'd always been so surly around him. She didn't want to be just another conquest to him. She wanted to be different. Important.

You're just another one-night stand, she told herself.

No, this didn't feel like that. Maybe she was lying to herself, but somehow this felt right.

She surrendered herself to his licks until she couldn't stand it anymore. She had to taste him too.

He actually whimpered as she moved away from him.

Rhea took a deep breath. She'd gone too far to stop now and she knew it. There was no way she could go back to just being a woman in the office where he was concerned.

She wanted more than that from him. Much more.

Her hand shaking in apprehension, she pulled her makeshift blindfold off him.

Those searing blue eyes captured and held hers. His eyes blazed with passion and need.

He was splendid.

And he was hers. At least for this afternoon.

Ace licked his lips as he watched her. He'd never been more aroused in his life and he had yet to even touch her.

Her gaze locked to his, he frowned as she left the bed until she pulled her G-string off. Oh, yeah, now that was definitely what he wanted.

She leaned over him and skimmed the bottoms over his chest, teasing him with it until she reached his cock.

Her eyes still on his, she climbed up on the bed, then took him into her mouth.

Ace ground his teeth as pleasure assailed him. Not just from the sensation of her mouth on him, but from the sight of her tasting him.

How many times had he dreamed this? How many times had he glimpsed a peek of her upper thigh in her cube, then got so hard for her that he'd almost wanted to go to the bathroom and jack off just for peace of mind?

Now she was making love to him. And it was better than anything he'd ever imagined.

"Untie me, Rhea. I want to touch you."

She took him all the way into her mouth and caressed his sack before she pulled back and finally gave in to his wishes.

Ace moaned ever so slightly at finally being free. His muscles protested a bit from all the inactivity.

But he didn't listen to them while he had Rhea in this bed. Grabbing her, he pulled her to his lips for a kiss.

Rhea sank into his arms. There was no other word for it. She felt so incredibly safe and warm here. Cocooned by his power.

She wrapped her body around his, wanting to absorb as much of his strength as she could. He felt wonderful!

She rubbed herself against all his hardness, wanting to feel every inch of his body against hers.

"Wait," Ace said, his voice raged. "Do you have a condom?"

Did she?

Rhea panicked as she realized what they had almost done. She wasn't on the pill, and to be honest she'd been so hot for him that she was glad he had come to his senses.

Truly she was grateful.

"I'm not sure." And she wasn't. It'd been a long time since she'd been with a man. "Do you?"

"No," he groaned. "I don't make it a habit of traveling with them."

That made her feel even better. At least he wasn't one of those "on the make" guys who kept one in his wallet "just in case."

"Hang on, let me go see if I can find one."

Ace let her up.

Rhea raced to the bathroom and started looking through her drawers.

"Come on," she said under her breath as she searched. She had to have one somewhere in here.

Please!

She felt his presence an instant before she heard his sharp intake of breath.

"You have the nicest ass I've ever seen."

Rhea backed up out of her cabinet to look up at him. "Thanks."

He knelt down beside her. "Can I help?"

"Yes. Hopefully there's one in here someplace."

"Good. You're no more prepared for this than I am." He gave her a scalding kiss before he pulled back and started searching frantically.

Rhea was about to give up before she finally found one. "Eureka!" she shouted in triumph.

The relief on his face was comical. "Oh, thank God."

Rhea leapt at him. She hit him so hard, she knocked him off-balance and they both tumbled into the hallway.

Ace laughed at her enthusiasm. "How long has it been since you had sex?"

"Let me put it to you this way: it was under the former administration."

"Ouch."

"You?"

"Not since Sheila gave me the heave-ho."

Sheila had been his last girlfriend, who had left him unexpectedly a little over a year ago. "Why did she leave you anyway?"

"Honestly?"

"Yes."

"I called her Rhea while we were having sex."

His words rang in her ears and she wasn't quite sure she'd heard them correctly. "What?"

He reached up and cupped her face in his hands. "You really don't know how much I've been wanting you, do you?"

No, and all this sounded too good to be real. "Why didn't you ever ask me out?"

"I was afraid you'd say no. At least this way, I had the comfort of believing you didn't find me a complete asshole. If I asked you out and you said no, then I'd know you didn't like me."

That didn't sound like the Ace she knew so well. "But you're not afraid of anything."

The look in his eyes seared her. She saw his heart. His soul. Most of all, she saw his sincerity. "That's so not true, Rhea."

Her heart soared at his words, but she was still hesitant. She'd been lied to too many times in the past. "Are you feeding me a complete line of bull?"

"Considering the fact that I let you tie me virtually naked to your bed in front of a complete stranger just so I could be with you, what do you think?"

"I think I wish you'd asked me out a long time ago."

Ace hissed as she bent down and kissed him. This was a

dream come true. Deepening his kiss, he reached for the condom and took it from her.

She immediately took it back. "I'll do it."

His heart racing, he watched as she tore the package open and pulled it out. The plastic was cold against him as she fit it over his cock and slowly unrolled it down the length of him. It was all he could do not to come just from the sensation of her hands on him.

But he didn't want this over with anytime soon. He wanted this to last.

His entire body on fire, he trailed his hand up the inside of her silken thigh until he reached the damp curls between her legs. She met his eyes as he slid his fingers down her cleft, carefully separating her folds and touching her for the very first time.

She was beautiful and her slick, soft flesh felt incredible to him. He couldn't wait to take her.

Biting her lip, she gently rubbed herself against his fingers as he sank one deep inside her body. It was the most incredible moment of his life. Probably because he'd dreamed of touching her more than he'd ever dreamed of any other woman.

It seemed as if he had waited his entire life for this one moment.

He ran his fingers over her, letting her wetness coat his fingers as he imagined what was to come. Of sinking himself deep inside her.

She moved forward. Ace leaned back as she crawled up his body.

Rhea couldn't wait to have him inside her. She straddled his waist, then slid herself back until she felt his hard, probing tip pressing against the part of her that was aching and throbbing most for his touch.

Ace lifted his hips and slid himself in all the way to his hilt.

She cried out in pleasure at the fullness of him inside her. "Ace," she choked, rocking herself against him. It felt so good to have him there.

He gripped her hips as he met her strokes and drove himself even deeper inside her.

Ace watched her in awe as she took control of their pleasure. His little uptight agent was as wild as any woman he'd ever slept with.

No, she was better.

She braced her hands against his chest as she ground herself against him in time to his rapid heartbeat. Leaning his head up, he took her breast into his mouth while he continued to hold her waist.

He licked and teased the taut peak, letting the roughness of it please his tongue.

Rhea couldn't think straight as she felt Ace with every molecule of her body. He was so much more than she had ever thought. He touched her like a man who actually cared for her, and it had been a long, long time since she'd felt that.

They made love furiously until her body couldn't take any more. Crying out, she fell forward onto his chest and let her release claim her. All she could hear was his heart pounding while the scent of him filled her senses.

Ace growled at the sensation of her body grasping his. He quickened his strokes as she continued to climax until he found his own moment of pure bliss.

His breathing ragged, he held her close to his chest where their hearts pounded together while his body spent itself inside her. In all honesty, he didn't want this moment to end.

It was perfect.

The feeling of her head against his chest. Her body molded to his. Her breath tickling his nipple.

If he lived an eternity, he would never know anything better than the feeling of Rhea in his arms.

Rhea closed her eyes as her heart finally slowed to a normal rate. The warmth of his body seeped into hers. In all her days of bantering with Ace, she'd never have guessed he would be like this. So tender and loving after sex.

He didn't seem to be in any hurry to get up, and the floor couldn't be all that comfortable for him.

"So what's on the menu for tomorrow?" he asked.

She laughed at that. "I'm not sure. What are you thinking?"

"I need more condoms."

"Ugh!" She pushed herself up to look down at him. "Do you ever have anything else on your mind?'"

"Food. But that only lasts about as long as it takes me to get a steak."

She shook her head at him. "Stop playing on the bad stereotype."

"I am a bad stereotype so long as you're lying naked on me. How on earth am I supposed to think about anything else?"

As she started to pull away, he stopped her with a fierce, hungry kiss that set every hormone in her body on fire again. This man had a mouth that was pure magic.

He pulled back, but left his hand buried in her hair. "Thank you, Rhea," he said sincerely, his gaze burning into hers.

"You're very welcome."

Reluctantly, she moved off him and headed back into the bathroom for the shower. "Want to join me?"

He gave her a hot once-over. "Pinocchio. There's no way I can go in there and not have another round. Since there's no more condoms . . ."

He was right. "Okay, I'll just be a minute."

Turning around, she shut the door and grabbed a towel out of her cabinet.

Rhea was still amazed that she wasn't more self-conscious around him. This wasn't like her and yet she felt so comfortable with him that it was almost terrifying.

She showered quickly, then opened the curtain to find Ace leaning against her bathroom vanity. He was hard again.

"Did you know you can see a perfect outline of your body when you're in there?"

"No."

He moved forward and nuzzled her neck before he gently licked the sensitive flesh right below her ear. "I can't believe what you do to me," he breathed in her ear, sending chills over her body.

He kissed her cheek, gave a light grope to her breast, then released her and entered her shower as she left it.

Rhea was so aroused that it was all she could do not to rip open the curtain and pin him to her shower wall.

He was more tempting than any man had a right to be.

But neither one of them needed her to get pregnant.

Forcing herself to dress, Rhea went to her bedroom. By the time she was dressed and had remade the bed, Ace joined her.

"Thinking of new ways to torture me?" he asked as she unfastened the restraints.

She opened her mouth to respond, but the sight of him wet, wearing nothing but a white towel, made all rational thoughts flee.

"You have to stop looking at me like that, Rhea."

"Like what?"

"Like I'm a piece of chocolate you're dying to taste. It gives me a hard-on every time."

She could easily see the proof of that statement. "Sorry, but it would help if you didn't parade yourself around naked in my presence."

He indicated his clothes, which were on her dresser, as he crossed the room to stand before her. "It's not exactly my fault."

"Oh, in that case, I better leave you alone while you put your clothes on."

"I'd rather you not."

She nibbled his chin before she pulled away. "If we don't stop, we're going to do something that could get us into serious trouble."

"I know," he whispered. "Okay, time for clothes."

Before she could leave the room, his cell phone rang. Ace picked it up and answered it.

"Hey, Joe." Ace cast an amused look at her, then winked. "No, obviously I'm not tied up since I answered the phone. . . . Thanks. So what do you need?"

Anxious as to why Joe might be calling, she moved forward, hoping to overhear something.

"Yeah, we'll be right there." He hung up.

"What's going on?"

"Joe just got word that Bender's sent out a call to his clients. Apparently he's found an abandoned arsenal of old Soviet weapons, including some nuclear. We need to get to the office for a briefing."

That succeeded in stifling her renegade passion. "I'll be waiting by the door."

Ace nodded and reached for his pants while she left him alone. Today had been a major mistake. He knew it.

As agents, they were supposed to stay detached, especially from each other. But after this morning, he wasn't feeling detached from Rhea.

Then again, he'd never been detached from her.

In fact, he was feeling extremely possessive. The thought of a bastard like Bender seeing her in that dominatrix outfit was almost enough to send him over the edge.

He didn't want anyone to see her like that. Anyone but him.

And how could he send her in there with a madman now?

Oh, this wasn't good. He'd never felt like this for another woman.

"Get a grip." He buttoned his pants, then reached for his shirt.

The two of them had a mission and he wasn't about to let one sexual encounter ruin it.

At least he hoped he didn't.

CHAPTER FOUR

"*I* knew it! Look at them. Did I not tell you that all that sniping was because they were seriously attracted to each other?"

Joe looked up at Tee's words to see Rhea and Ace through the two-way mirror of his office. Damn, Tee had been right. They were making goo-goo eyes at each other.

"Shit," he said under his breath.

"What?" Tee asked innocently.

"Work and play don't mix."

Tee gave him an arched look. "Since when?"

"Since we have to send her in practically naked to beat information out of an arm's dealer. Given the way Ace is eyeballing her, I don't think he's going to approve."

"What has that got to do with anything? Ace is a good enough agent to do what he has to."

"Yeah, right."

Tee gave Joe an angry frown. "You and I are best friends, and how many times have you sent me into danger?"

"That's because you're the Dragon Lady. You'd take the head off anyone dumb enough to cross you."

She cocked her head at him and spoke pointedly, "I haven't killed *you* yet."

"Not from lack of trying on your part, and personally, I'd rather you kill me than make me sit down and talk to your mom. That woman hates my guts with an unfounded reasoning."

"You keep talking like that about my mother, Joe Public, and I just might make sure that your automatic car payment gets misrouted." She looked back at Rhea and Ace. "Trust me. This'll be fine."

Now it was Joe's turn to scoff. "The last time I trusted you, I got three bullets in my back."

"No, you got shot because you trusted me and then you didn't listen to what I said and did your own stupid thing."

He mocked her by screwing up his face and repeating her words back at her.

"That's it. I'm emailing my mother to come have lunch here tomorrow."

"No!" Joe snapped, immediately contrite. "She makes me crazy. She won't even speak English when I'm around and I know she speaks it better than I do."

"We will finish this later," Tee snapped before she opened the door to let Ace and Rhea in.

Ace looked a bit sheepish as he came to stand in front of Joe's desk, while Rhea took a seat in the black leather chair in front of it.

"So how was your morning?" Tee asked as she came to

lean against the side of the desk. "Did Beullah do her job?"

Ace nodded. "Oh, yeah. They hog-tied me in a manner to make you proud, Tee."

"Good. Pity they let you up."

Ignoring her, Ace looked at Joe. "So what's the new information?"

Joe shuffled through a couple of folders. "Bender's on the move. You two are going to have to head out to Germany tonight."

Both Ace and Rhea gaped.

"What?" Ace asked.

"You heard him," Tee said. "I already have your flight booked."

The news went over Ace like sandpaper. "She can't go in alone. She hasn't had time to prepare herself yet. Hell, she barely knows what she's doing."

"Excuse me?" Rhea asked, her tone extremely offended. "I think I should have beat you harder."

He glared at her.

"Don't worry, Ace." Tee pulled an envelope off Joe's desk. "You're going in as Hermann the towel boy."

"Pardon?"

Joe tossed Ace a passport. "You and Dieter will be right outside the room, listening in case she needs backup. Retter will be on recording detail along with Dagmar. There shouldn't be any trouble you guys can't handle. God knows you've all had worse."

Tee handed the entire file to Ace. "You two are technically on vacation for the next few days while Rhea learns her stuff over in Germany. I've ordered some training DVDs for you to study so that you can learn how to beat him black-and-blue. Bender that is, not Ace."

Rhea nodded. "Okay."

"We don't know when Bender is going to show up, looking for Ute," Joe said. "But according to Ute, he always gets feisty right before a big coup, and his latest find definitely qualifies. I figure you guys have three days to a week before he shows himself. What do you think, Ace? You know him better than anyone."

"You're right," he said. "He usually books time with Ute the night before he pulls off his shit. We need to get over there and be ready."

"Then you two go ahead. Retter is already in Germany and waiting for your orders. The rest of us will follow you over there on a later flight."

Ace handed Rhea her passport and printout for her plane ticket, then led the way out of Joe's office.

"You don't think they suspect anything, do you?" Rhea asked in a hushed tone as soon as they were out of hearing range.

On the way over here, they had decided that it would be business as usual for them so that no one else in the office would know what had happened.

God help them if any of the losers here ever learned they'd had sex. They would tease them to the point they'd have to kill someone.

Ace glanced back over his shoulder. "Joe's pretty dense.

Tee . . . I don't know. I swear sometimes that woman can read minds."

"Oh, don't say that. That makes me nervous."

"Yeah," he agreed. "So how do we handle the next few days?"

"Well, normally we'd do deep, intrinsic training . . ."

Ace couldn't stop the grin that took over his face. "I was hoping you'd say that."

She shook her head at his enthusiasm. At times he was simply evil.

But she was glad this was one of those times.

Once they reached Germany, they spent night and day together. Rhea was stunned at how comfortable she became around Ace while she was completely naked. It was liberating to have no sense of being body conscious around him.

How could she when he seemed to prefer her that way?

"I'm supposed to be training with you tied up," she said as Ace secured her hands, which were tied together to her headboard.

"Turnabout is fair play."

She supposed it was.

"What are you doing?" she asked as he took one ankle carefully in his hand.

He kissed the sole of her foot.

Rhea moaned as he moved to lick her toes and to torment them one by one until she was squirming.

"I'm having my way with you, princess." He tied her foot to the bedpost.

After he had the other leg secured, Ace stood back. He'd never thought about tying someone up as being particularly sexy, but he had to admit the sight of her tied and waiting for him turned him on a lot more than he would ever have guessed.

He slid his briefs off, then pouted slightly. "I should have tied you down on your back."

"Too late."

"Not necessarily." Grinning at her, Ace slid himself slowly up under her.

Rhea hissed at the feeling of him there. She was completely open and exposed to his every desire.

She dipped her head down to kiss him while he slid his hands down her back to gently cup her butt and press her hips to his. She could feel him growing hard against her stomach.

"Hmmm," he breathed, rubbing himself against her. "What have I found?"

Rhea sucked her breath in sharply as his rough fingers gently prodded her clit.

"You do know, I'm getting entirely too attached to you, Ace?"

"Yeah," he said as he slid one long, lean finger inside her. "And I know that I should get up, get dressed, and go to my room."

But he didn't move to get up and that thrilled her most of all.

"Why aren't you leaving?" she asked.

"Honestly?"

She nodded.

"I'm desperate for you, Rhea." He pulled his hand away from her, then brushed the hair back from her face so that he could look at her. "I've been desperate to taste your body since the day you first came into the office, stumbled, and fell, flashing me those little pink panties you had on under your skirt."

Her face flushed with heat. "You saw that?"

"Oh, yeah, and I've dreamed of nothing but peeling those pink panties off of you ever since."

"And now that you have?"

"I want the right to keep peeling them off you anytime you make me hot."

She rolled her eyes at him. "That is without a doubt the most unromantic thing I have ever heard, and if I wasn't tied down, I'd leave."

He laughed low in his throat as his hand returned to stroke her between her legs. "Then it's a good thing I tied you down first, huh?"

It was hard to think straight while he touched her like this. While his fingers stroked and circled her.

"Tell me what you want, Rhea."

"I want you inside me."

Ace gave her a fierce kiss, then moved his lips slowly down her body to her breasts, where he took his time teasing her. Then lower and lower while her body burned for him. He licked his way to her thigh, then nipped her hip as he slid completely out from under her.

Rhea tried to look over her shoulder but couldn't see anything.

She felt the bed dip with his weight as he moved to lean over her.

He brushed the hair back from her neck before he nibbled at her earlobe. She shook all over as his tongue teased her ear. His breath scorched her.

He slid his hand around her hip, to sink it deep in her fold before he entered her.

Rhea gasped as pleasure assaulted her.

Ace was blinded by the sensation of her warm, wet heat. He could lose himself inside her forever.

But today was their last day to play. Tomorrow Bender would show himself.

One of them could die. It wasn't something agents gave much thought to, but as he rode her slowly, that fear finally found him.

What if something went wrong?

"Ace? Are you okay?"

He placed a kiss to her cheek. "I'm fine, baby."

Rhea moaned as his fingers stroked her while he thrust deep inside her. Still, she could tell something was different about him in spite of what he said. There was a hesitancy to his touch. A reservation.

But she didn't have long to contemplate that before her orgasm claimed her.

Ace held her tight, his fingers working their magic until the very last tremor had been coaxed out of her.

A few heartbeats later she felt him tense as he too joined her in bliss.

Rhea lay there with his weight pleasantly crushing her while he untied her hands.

"I'm going to miss our 'training' sessions."

"I'll bet you will," she said with a laugh.

He moved to the side of her so that she could roll over and snuggle close.

Tenderly, he brushed the hair back from her face.

Rhea sighed. "I wish we could go back and do the last few days over."

"Yeah, me too. But you know, this doesn't have to end . . . does it?"

Rhea swallowed at his question. "I don't know, Ace. A relationship is hard enough. But between two agents . . ."

"Dagmar and Dieter make it work."

That was true. The two of them were married, and to Rhea's knowledge they'd never had so much as a hiccup in their relationship.

He took her hand in his and moved it to his lips so that he could nibble her palm. "Can we at least try?"

She smiled at him. What woman could say no to that look? "Okay."

Ace returned her smile before he kissed her on the brow. But in the back of his mind, he couldn't shake the sensation that something was going to go seriously wrong tomorrow.

CHAPTER FIVE

*A*ce was in position, waiting with Dieter while Rhea dressed herself for the arrival of Bender. It had taken some doing to get the PussyCat Club to "hire" Rhea, but after a nice long talk with the German authorities, the owner decided it would be in her best interest to let Rhea do her job.

Now Rhea was in a locker room that the dominatrixes used to garb themselves in their work attire while Ace and Dieter were outside in the blood red hallway that led to all the "service" rooms.

"Are you all right, Krux?" Dieter asked as they stacked towels onto a cart so that to any passersby, they would look like two regular workers restocking the towels for the clients.

Dieter was a tall, extremely muscular, blond German native. He'd been recruited by Joe a little over a year ago and since then had been quite an asset to their team. Having been born and bred in Europe, Dieter knew every back hole and dive in six countries. Better still, he had questionable associates who often leaked vital information to them.

Ace could feel a tic working in his jaw. "No. I don't like sending her in there alone with a psycho."

"Relax. But I know what you mean. Dagmar never listens to me either. She is"—he paused as if searching for the foreign English word—"stubborn. Many times she goes when she should stay. But Rhea is more cautious. She knows what to do. I don't think we have anything to worry over with that one."

Yeah, but Ace really hated the thought of her tying Bender down. The beating part he could live with. It was the "other" unknown variables that had his stomach knotted.

"Excuse me?" an extremely well-built, leather-clad mistress said in German as she came into the hallway from a room three doors down. "What is it you two do? You need to be working at getting these towels to the room and not dawdling with idle chatter."

"*Ja,* we're working," Dieter responded, knowing that Ace's German was flawless, but accented enough to give him away as a foreigner.

"You," the mistress said, indicating Dieter. "I need you standing by room five after Herr Bender leaves."

Ace's heart stopped beating.

"Why?" Dieter asked.

She sighed heavily. "He always leaves his woman a mess. We will need to get Bettie to our doctor as soon as he goes, and you look more than strong enough to carry her."

"Pardon?" Ace asked as his sight turned dim.

"*Ja,* he is not a good man, but he pays us well."

"But I thought he was the one who liked to be tied up," Dieter said.

She laughed as if the very idea amused her. "Who told you such? *Nein,* he would never allow anyone else to tie him up." She cracked the small riding crop in her hand at them. *"Schnell, schnell.* He will be here momentarily."

Neither of them moved until after she'd entered a room on the left.

"We were fed bullshit," Ace said from between clenched teeth.

He grabbed his cell phone from his pocket and buzzed Retter, who was in the building across the street with the recording equipment. "We have a problem, Retter. My informer lied. Bender doesn't get beaten. He does the beating."

"What?"

Ace clenched the phone so hard his hand was shaking. "You heard me. What do we do?"

He could hear Joe in the background telling Retter what to do after Retter had filled him in on what was happening. "It's too late to call this off without blowing our covers. Rhea will just have to go through it."

Ace saw red. "Hell, no."

He hung up while Retter started to yell at him.

"What did he say?" Dieter asked.

"Something I didn't want to hear. I'm pulling Rhea out."

"If Retter said—"

Ace cut Dieter's words off with a staggering punch that rendered him unconscious. Ace grabbed the huge bear of a man and shoved him into the towel closet, covered him with towels, then shut and locked the door.

God help him, Dieter would beat the shit out him later.

But that was later.

Right now he had a damsel who was about to get seriously distressed.

Rhea was checking out her stockings in the mirror when the door to her dressing room opened. She frowned as she saw Ace.

By the look on his face, she could tell something was wrong. "What's up?"

"I'm getting you out of here."

"Why?"

"Bender is a psycho and he is going to beat you. Not the other way around."

Rhea went pale at this disclosure. "What did Retter say?"

"I don't give a shit what he said. Retter is an idiot and I'm not going to send you in there so that fat bastard can mangle you. This is my case and I'm—"

"This is my job, Ace. It's what I do."

Ace cursed in frustration. "Will no one listen to reason?"

Narrowing her gaze at him, she put her hands on her hips to let him know that she thought he was the one being unreasonable. "Ace, we have to nail this bastard. If he confesses—"

"And if the bitch lied about who gets beaten, doesn't it stand to reason that she lied about the confession bit as well?"

"Maybe she didn't. We have to get this guy off the street, and if this is the way, then this is the way."

That didn't make a bit of sense to him. "Fine, I'll kill him and we—"

"We're not assassins, Ace. We work by law and order."

His fury roiled through him at that. "You don't know Tee very well, do you? I hate to be the messenger, Rhea, but Tee is a cold-blooded killer."

"Oh, please."

Rhea started for the door.

Unable to stand by and watch her be hurt, Ace ran for her. He grabbed her before she could stop him.

"What are you doing?"

He pulled the handcuffs out of his backpocket that he was supposed to reserve for Bender and slapped them over her wrists.

"Ace!" She tried to squirm out from his hold.

He took the scarf from her neck and used it to gag her. "I'm sorry, Rhea. I can't let you do this. You're right. Someone has to go in there. But by God, it won't be you."

Picking her up, he carried her to a locker and set her inside even while she fought against him.

Rhea was furious. Ace could see it plainly in her brown eyes as he shut the door and locked it. But it was better she be pissed than dead.

"All right, Krux," he said to himself under his breath. "It's time to do the nasty."

Personally, he'd rather be dead, but what was a little dignity compared to Rhea's life?

★   ★   ★

"Well, it worked for Tim Curry." Ace surveyed himself with a critical eye. He definitely wouldn't win a beauty pageant. With any luck, Bender might even be half-blind.

Or half-drunk.

It was dark in the rooms . . . maybe Bender wouldn't notice much.

Maybe.

"I am so fired," he muttered. But it would be worth it.

He hoped.

Pulling his garter belt straight, he headed down the hallway to the room where Bender should be waiting.

Sure enough, the man was there. He had on a long, black PVC coat with buckles and straps that looked strangely close to a straitjacket. At least the man did have on a pair of glasses. Maybe he would be blind as a bat.

"Who are you?" Bender asked in German, curling his lip as he surveyed Ace with a disgusted look.

"Latex . . . Bettie." Ace tried not to cringe at the latter as he kept his voice high and singsongy in an effort to mimic some kind of European accent while he spoke German. Hell, he hadn't been born in Hollywood for nothing.

He would just remember that this was to save Rhea and all the other innocent victims Bender intended to prey upon.

Bender cocked his head. "You don't look like Bettie Page."

Ace put his hands on his hips and feigned indignation. "And you don't look like Brad Pitt, but notice I'm not complaining."

Bender gave him an arched glare. "You are uppity. I like that in a woman. Now show me your tits."

Yeah, right.

"How about first we see yours?"

Before Bender could leave or call for help, Ace seized him, ripped his coat, and pulled it down on his arms so that he was bound and unable to move.

"Ah," Ace said with a tsk in his faked accent. "You have not been working out, Herr Bender. What do you do that you are so weak in the arms?"

"See here, I—"

"Shh," Ace said, cutting him off. "Bettie will take care of you, *Schatz.*" Provided "Bettie" didn't toss her cookies in revulsion. "Tell her what you want done to you."

Hopefully it involved a bullwhip and this guy's ass on the floor.

Bender shouted furiously, "Let me go!"

"Nein, nein. You have paid for the hour of domination and an hour you will get. Now tell Bettie what she wants to hear."

Rhea was ready to choke the life out of Ace by the time the door to her locker was opened.

She looked out to see Retter, who whistled low.

"Nice outfit, Rhea."

She glared at him as he removed her gag.

"Where the hell is he?" she snapped.

"Up shit creek."

"Good. Now give me the paddle so I can beat him with it."

Retter laughed as he unlocked the cuffs.

Rhea rubbed her sore wrists as she continued to glare at Retter. At six-four, he was every bit as handsome as Ace, but nowhere near to dying as Ace was at the moment.

Just wait until she got her hands on him.

"He blew it, didn't he?" she asked.

Retter set the cuffs aside. "Yes and no."

"What do you mean yes and no?"

"I think your boyfriend has quite a future as a dominatrix."

Rhea frowned, but Retter didn't elaborate. Instead, he handed her his jacket, then led her out into the hallway where there were several German agents along with Joe and members of the CIA and Interpol.

"What's going on here?" she asked Joe. "Where's Ace?"

"In custody."

Her stomach clenched. "Custody? Whose? For what?"

"Ours," Retter said. "For being the ugliest transvestite in the history of humanity. I swear, we ought to be allowed to kill Bender for sheer, blind stupidity alone."

Rhea was even more confused. "What?"

"Ace went in as you, or rather as Latex Bettie," Joe explained.

Her heart stopped beating at the thought of Ace trying to pose as a woman. Yeah, right! Ace would never pass as a female. He was far too masculine.

"Oh, no. Did Bender get away?"

"No," Joe said. "We got him, along with a full confession."

Rhea gaped. "How?"

Retter let out a deep, evil laugh. "Latex Bettie wields a mean whip. He had Bender spilling more guts than a kosher butcher."

"So why is Ace in custody then?" Rhea asked.

"Mostly for pissing me off by not following orders," Joe said in a surly tone. "He's lucky I don't let the German authorities keep him."

Retter gave a crooked grin. "I can arrange that, if you want."

"Don't tempt me."

"Can I see him?" Rhea asked.

"Trust me," Retter said. "You don't want to see him. Think Frank-N-Furter gone bad. Real bad."

Why was it every time Retter spoke, he only confused her more. "Frank-N-Furter?"

"Rocky Horror Picture Show." He shuddered.

"C'mon," Joe said, leading her away from Retter. "I have Ace in a room down here."

She followed Joe down the garish hallway to a small room where Dieter sat with a cold pack held to his jaw while Dagmar stroked his hair.

Dieter glared at them. "I'm going to kill him, Joe."

"I know, Dieter, hang around and I might authorize it."

"If you don't," Dagmar snapped, "I will. How dare he hit my Dieter. I want his tenticles cut off."

Rhea had a bad feeling Dagmar meant *testicles,* but in the mood the Czech woman was in, Rhea wasn't about to correct her.

Joe opened another door in the rear of the room, which

led to one of the theme rooms. It was a garish red, gauzy place that looked even tackier under the bright fluorescent lights that were only turned on for cleaning.

Ace sat on a bench with his back to her. His hands were cuffed behind him.

And he looked awful.

"Oh, good grief," Rhea said as she surveyed the mess that was Ace dressed in a PVC teddy and fishnets. The black wig on his head did nothing for his features, which were outlined in grotesque, overdone makeup. He looked like a cross between Gloria Swanson and Bozo the clown. "If Bender thought for one minute that you were a woman, I am seriously offended on behalf of every member of my gender."

Ace turned around to see her. "You okay?"

"Her?" Joe asked disgustedly. "It's your own ass you should be worried about, Krux."

Still, Ace's concern for her made her strangely weepy.

Ace's intense blue gaze never left hers. "Before you fire me, shoot me, or hand me over to German custody, could you give me a few minutes alone with her, Joe?"

"Sure." He walked out and shut the door.

Part of Rhea wanted to kill Ace for what he'd done. "Why did you do this, Ace?"

He frowned at her. "Don't you know?"

"No. I can appreciate the fact that you didn't want me hurt, but this is what I do. It's what *we* do. You can't just go off half-cocked and pull a stunt like this. What if Bender had gotten away?"

Ace let out a tired breath. "Look, Rhea, I never wanted

to feel like this about anyone. But there was no way on earth I could have stood there and let that bastard hit you. I don't care if they lock me up for the rest of eternity, I will never allow another man to hurt the woman I love. So I figured it was either this or I kill him."

Rhea couldn't breathe as she heard those words. It couldn't be true. "You don't love me, Ace. How could you?"

He looked aghast at her. "Look at me, Rhea. Do you think anything other than love would *ever* have me in this godforsaken outfit?"

Tears welled in her eyes as she closed the distance between them. "Really?"

"Yes, baby, really. You're all I've ever wanted."

How could any woman ever hold that against a man? Cupping his face in her hands, Rhea kissed him soundly. She broke off the kiss a few seconds later, laughing.

"What?"

"You have no idea how confusing it is to kiss a man dressed as a woman."

He grimaced at that. "I don't know how you wear this stuff. The hose alone are killing me."

Laughing, she pulled the wig off his head and unlocked the cuffs.

Ace seized her then and held her close as his tongue explored every inch of her mouth. Rhea sighed at the kiss and held him tight.

She laughed again. "You look so ugly as a woman."

He joined her laughter. "Yeah. This stuff definitely looks better on you."

The door to the room swung open.

"Ugh!" Joe snapped. "I'm blind *and* repulsed."

Rhea tried to move away, but Ace held her close.

"What do you want, Joe?" he asked gruffly.

"I only wanted to remind you that this room is wired and we're still recording everything the two of you are saying."

"Did you hear?" Rhea asked.

"Every word, and I have to say that in all the years I've known Ace, I've never known him to say that to another living woman, except for his mother." He shook his head at them. "Fine, Ace. Since we got Bender, I'm going to let you off this time. But if you ever do this stunt again . . ."

"I know. You'll cut off my tenticles."

Rhea laughed at Ace's imitation of Dagmar.

"Exactly. Now as you two were. Just don't forget you have a debriefing in an hour and a plane to catch in three." Joe started out of the room.

"Hey, Joe," Ace called.

Joe paused.

"Thanks, bud. I owe you."

Joe nodded, then quietly left.

Ace gave her a devilish grin. "So, we have an hour . . ."

Cocking her head with attitude, Rhea stepped back and seized a whip.

"What are you doing?"

She cracked the whip near him. "I want to make an honest woman of you, Ace."

"Huh?"

"Get on your knees and propose."

Ace laughed. "You're not serious?"

"Are you?"

He sobered. "Yeah. For the first time in my life, I am." Without hesitating, he got down on his knees. "Rhea, will you marry me?"

"I dunno. Now that you're proposing, I really have to think about this. . . . Transvestites really aren't my thing." She walked over to him and brushed his hair back from his forehead. "Do you promise to never again interfere with my job?"

"I can only promise that I will do my best. I know you're capable, I do. But you have to understand that emotions don't always think before they act."

That was true enough. Rhea doubted if she could ever stand by and let him be hurt either. She would have done the same exact thing had their roles been reversed. "Okay, we'll take it on a case-by-case basis."

"Thank you."

Rhea shuddered as one of his false eyelashes came free. "Can you at least promise me that you'll never, ever wear that outfit again?"

"Definitely."

She nodded. "Then fine. I can marry you."

Ace grinned and rose to his feet. He lifted her up in his arms and headed for the door.

Before he could open it, Rhea stopped him. "By the way, just for the sake of clarification, *I* will be the one in the wedding dress, correct?"

"No doubt about it. Now I have to go get out of this outfit before we hit debriefing."

Rhea gave him a playful look. "So does this mean I get to see you naked?"

"Yes, ma'am, it certainly does."

PROMISE ME FOREVER

Melanie George

CHAPTER ONE

The Bombers were up by seven, with two and a half minutes left on the clock. The Cowboys could still win it with an eleventh-hour comeback, but the chances seemed slim that they would.

Donovan surveyed the field, deaf to the roar of the crowd. Forty-five thousand fans chanted his name, but he heard nothing.

He felt that familiar surge of adrenaline, a rush of atmospheric pressure. White Lightning, the press had dubbed him. A phenomenon. And at that moment, he felt like one.

His moves were liquid as he threw the football down the field like a bullet, his arm on fire from the force of the pass—followed a split second later by a crushing tackle as the Cowboys' defense propelled him back to the thirty-yard line in what seemed like slow motion, his entire life flashing before his eyes as he slammed into the ground with brutal force, the breath knocked from his lungs. Searing pain radiated up his right side before darkness descended in blessed relief.

*   *   *

Donovan's eyes snapped open, his heart hammering. It took him a moment to realize that he was no longer on the field but in bed, and not in Detroit but back home in Mississippi.

He rubbed his eyes. Christ, even now, two years later, that cold Sunday in January was as vivid as the day it had happened.

He sucked in a deep breath and stared up at the ceiling, watching the paddles of the fan swing above his head, a layer of sweat coating his naked body.

Out of habit he flexed his right arm, still feeling a twinge of pain. A year of physical therapy had given him a working arm, but not a throwing arm; it had been broken too badly. A career-ending injury for a quarterback.

The White Lightning was gone forever, and with the end of the only life he had ever known and the only thing he had ever truly done well came a bleak emptiness that nothing had been able to fill. Alcohol and a string of meaningless affairs had managed to keep the void inside him at bay.

He tried to sit up but the room began to spin, forcefully reminding him that he had overindulged. *Again.* He'd eventually be an outstanding drunk at the rate he was going. Anything done in excess had a dulling effect over time, or so he'd heard. He figured he'd test the theory.

Gripping the edge of the mattress, he swung his legs over the side and acclimated himself to an upright position, waiting for his alcohol-saturated brain to float toward functioning consciousness.

Christ, how many shots of tequila had he downed? Five? Six? Twenty?

"Damn," he groaned. "Still alive."

He should be able to hold his liquor better than this. In high school, he could party with the best of 'em and still kick ass in football practice the next day. Even in college at good old Mississippi State, he could tie one on and stay loose.

Playing ball had been what he had always wanted, what he had worked his whole life for. But the dream had come to an abrupt and painful end during that last game of the play-off season, nearly eight years to the day after the wild ride had begun.

He had learned to coexist with the fate that had been doled out to him. But he had never come to grips with what he had thrown aside in his quest for the gold ring. The one thing he had truly wanted, he had left behind. The one person who had the power to topple him from that pinnacle.

Savannah.

Her name ran through his mind like an echoing plea for salvation. That's what she had been to him, but he hadn't realized it at the time.

Donovan forced back the image and pushed to his feet, steering himself toward the window, where the sun was just creeping over the mountaintops, a backdrop to the sleepy little town in the distance. He had been in such a rush to leave this place. How ironic that life had brought him full circle.

Bedsheets rustled, and he glanced over his shoulder at the naked female body sprawled across the spot where he had been lying only moments before. A mass of red hair spread across the pillow, and one extravagantly long leg twined in the sheets.

A fuzzy image surfaced of her sitting on his lap last night, pouring whiskey shooters down his throat while telling him that she sunbathed in the nude—and that she wasn't wearing any panties beneath her short skirt. What happened after that was a blur.

Donovan raked a hand through his hair and sighed. Most women were only interested in his money and didn't give a rat's ass about the Southern boy who had grown up impoverished and fought his way to the top.

Only one woman had really known him, had really cared, and he had foolishly let her slip through his fingers.

Donovan moved back to the bed and sat down on the edge, his bleary gaze taking in the remnants of a party. Half-empty glasses of Stoli and bone-dry bottles of Jack Daniel's littered the room.

He rubbed his hands over his face and lay down, remembering what, or rather who, had precipitated the party: his longtime friend and former teammate from the Bombers, Nick Stanton.

Nick had decided to surprise Donovan on his first day home by showing up at his door—to help him settle in, he'd claimed.

Nick's idea of settling in had turned into a twenty-four-hour alcoholic haze—and for that, Donovan intended to introduce his friend to his left and right fists, just as soon as the world stopped spinning.

The sun was just beginning its descent, its crimson-gold hue spreading over Savannah's farm, dappling the horses grazing in the distance with warm paint strokes. A rocking chair swayed gently in a southerly breeze that blew in over the mountains, the air carrying a hint of jasmine and pine.

She had always loved this time of day, when all was quiet and her mind had a chance to slow down and reflect.

But for two days she had not been able to find that peace. Donovan had come home, and everything seemed out of tilt with the world.

He had turned his back on Mississippi and her ten years ago, and she had believed her heart had healed. That she was over him for good. But deep down, some feelings yet remained. He had been her first love. And her first heartbreak.

"What'cha lookin' at Mom?"

Savannah glanced over her shoulder and smiled as her daughter, Reese, walked into the kitchen, swiping a wedge of the sliced apples Savannah had intended for a pie off a plate on the counter. She had picked the apples from her very own orchard.

Pushing away from the back-door screen, she moved to hug her daughter. Ruffling Reese's long, dark hair, she replied, "I was just watching the sunset."

Reese glanced around her mother and out the door. "It sure is pretty. I bet heaven is a lot like this, don't you?"

"I certainly hope so, sweetie." She kissed Reese's forehead and whisked an apple wedge from the plate, poking one in her own mouth. "So where's Uncle Frank?"

Frank was her older, and very protective, brother. Ever since Donovan had devastated her life, Frank had made a point of making sure no one ever did it again. He had interrogated, and run off, a number of potential boyfriends. But Savannah had never really minded. Until Jake, her heart had never been in it.

"He's still outside tinkering with that old tractor," Reese replied. "He swears he's going to get it to work any day now. He's been sayin' that for almost three years."

Savannah chuckled. "You know your uncle. He is dedicated to a cause."

Plopping herself down on top of the kitchen table with the remaining apple slices, Reese asked, "When will the new guests arrive?"

"Anytime now." Savannah's bed-and-breakfast was thriving and she could barely keep up with the demand, especially since her own life was changing. "I hope Janette has their rooms ready."

"Nope," Reese stated in an apple-muffled voice.

"What do you mean, nope?"

"I haven't seen Janette all day. I don't think she showed up."

Savannah stifled an irritated sigh. She didn't know why she had ever hired Janette Carlton. In the month since her regular housekeeper had retired, nothing had gone smoothly.

Janette had shown up one day in dire need of a job. Apparently being a part-time waitress and a full-time party girl didn't pay the bills.

Savannah had taken her on to try to help her out. She knew the girl's mother well. Daisy Carlton was a widow who had been struggling with multiple sclerosis while trying to raise three boys and one headstrong girl who had given her more angst than all her sons combined.

The decision to hire Janette proved more irksome every day. Not only did Savannah have a houseful of guests coming to The Oaks, but she also had visitors arriving for a very special event.

Her wedding.

Savannah could hardly believe tomorrow was the day. She had started dating Jake two years ago, but she had known him for five, and while she had always found him a sweet and devoted guy—and a man who, as a pediatrician, loved children, like her—she had not expected more to come of it. But one day he had kissed her on the front porch and it had been . . . comfortable and warm. Lacking the usual awkwardness of a first kiss.

Savannah glanced at the clock. Her husband-to-be was at the local strip club for a traditional bachelor party. He had been so cute in his avowals that he had no interest in a bachelor party and that if she didn't want him to go, he wouldn't.

She had silenced his worries with a smile and a kiss. Yes, she had heard about the things that could happen at a bachelor party, but she trusted Jake completely.

"Well," she sighed, "I guess I better get to cleaning up those rooms or we will have some very unhappy guests."

"Mom?" Reese queried, stopping Savannah as she headed out of the kitchen.

"Yes?"

Reese hesitated, her expression serious. "Do you think we'll be happy living with Jake? I mean, what about staying here? This is our home, after all."

The only home her daughter had ever known, Savannah thought as she walked over to Reese and cupped her cheeks, which still retained some of the roundness of childhood. "This will always be our home, honey. We're not giving it up, but we will be Jake's family now and he wants us with him."

Reese stared down at her socks, one yellow, one blue. "I know. I guess I'll just miss it here."

"You can still be here every day, just like now. And someday The Oaks will be yours and you can do with it whatever you like."

Reese nodded absently, then said after a moment of hesitation, "What about him?"

Savannah frowned. "Him?"

"The man Uncle Frank told me you once loved. He's come back, Uncle Frank said. Is it true?"

Savannah had not expected this line of questioning from her daughter. The subject was not one she cared to think about, let alone discuss, but Reese deserved the truth. "Yes, Donovan Jerricho has come home, and, yes, I once loved him. I don't know why your uncle would take it upon himself to tell you this." When she got her hands on Frank, she would brain him.

Reese looked embarrassed. "He didn't tell me, exactly. I heard him talking to Rufus."

Rufus Williams was an old high school buddy of Frank's, one Savannah had never particularly liked. He had always looked at her with far too much lechery in his eyes.

"What else did you hear Uncle Frank say?"

"He said that this man hurt you real bad and that he should have stayed where he was and never come back to Mississippi, and that if he thought he was going to cause any trouble, Uncle Frank would make him change his mind real quick."

Oh, boy. This was not what she needed right now. Why had she thought her brother would ignore Donovan's return? Frank was still a hothead. She had to speak to him before his emotions carried him away.

"Do you still love this guy, Mom?"

For a split second, Savannah couldn't form the words. "No," she managed. "It's long over. I'm marrying Jake, remember?" She smiled reassuringly, but it felt as though she was trying to reassure herself, as well. "Now, how about letting me see that smile?"

Reese gave a tentative lift of her lips. Savannah crossed her eyes and stuck out her tongue, prompting a laugh from her daughter.

"That's more like it. Now, come help me get the rooms ready. We've got a busy few days ahead of us."

Savannah took her daughter's hand and together they left the kitchen. But as they went up the steps leading to the guest wing, Savannah couldn't shake the nervous tension that had nothing to do with her impending nuptials, and everything to do with a certain ex–football player.

Chapter Two

*D*onovan awoke abruptly, his gaze shooting to the clock. Eight p.m. Damn, he'd fallen back asleep, and here he'd told his old high school buddy Meat that he would stop by The Jiggle Room, where Meat bartended, so that they could catch up on old times. He pointed his feet toward the bathroom, hoping a hot shower would rouse him.

An hour later, Donovan found himself with a drink in his hand before his ass hit the barstool. He gave his old high school chum an up-yours salute with his glass and took a swig.

Meat, otherwise known as Herschel Dubrowski, stood behind the bar staring at Donovan with a stupid grin that told Donovan his old friend was up to something he wasn't going to like.

He banged the glass down on the bar and coughed. "Jesus, what did you put in here? Acid?"

"I should have, you old shithead," Meat retorted in that slow drawl that made most people think he was 340 pounds of pure stupidity. He was a good three inches taller than Donovan at six-six, with arms and legs as stout as tree trunks and a belly that was the first thing that hit an opponent.

"So what took you so long?" Meat said, refilling Donovan's glass in preparation for another walloping hangover that he undoubtedly should avoid but wouldn't.

"I was detained by an unknown female in my bed."

Meat laughed, clearly not surprised. "That would be Janette."

"Somehow I suspect you know how she ended up there?"

Meat smiled broadly. "I gave her your address. Nick and I thought you might like some company. The gal does loves football players, even a broke-down cracker like you."

"This broke-down cracker can still kick your fat rump."

"You could never kick my fat rump. But I'll let you keep on deluding yourself."

A loud burst of laughter brought both men's gazes to the corner of the room. A tall, busty brunette was gyrating in front of some guy's chair, her body blocking him from view, but Donovan could see the guy's hands nervously clenching his Dockers-clad knees.

"Poor sucker is about to end life as he knows it," Donovan muttered, wondering why he felt so damn jealous of some schmo.

Ten years ago he had come close to marriage and had counted himself among the lucky at escaping. But age and time had brought other emotions.

"Interesting that you should find that guy so unfortunate," came a voice from behind him.

Donovan swiveled his head and eyed the hulking giant behind him. "The minute my skull stops throbbing, you're dead, so I'd advise you to start running now."

Nick Stanton let out a bark of laughter and pulled up the barstool next to Donovan. Nick had retired from the Bombers a year earlier. As a Heisman Trophy–winning offensive lineman, he had helped lead the Bombers to two Super Bowl wins.

"You always were a lot of hot air, Jerricho. But I promise to let you have at me when you're feeling competent enough to make a fist."

The sound of a commotion brought Donovan's gaze back to the bachelor party in the corner. Six men were cheering on the guy in the chair, who tightly clenched a ten-dollar bill.

The dancer lifted the edge of her skimpy G-string to entice him to put the money somewhere provocative. With an uproar of hurrahs, the soon-to-be-shackled bridegroom slipped the bill down the front of the girl's thong, earning him a near smothering with her boobs.

"One small step for womankind, one giant leap for male stupidity," Donovan said.

"If I didn't know better," Nick remarked with humor in his voice, "I might think that was bitterness I heard. Could it be you long for wedded bliss?"

"What I long for is peace," Donovan retorted. "Meat, don't you have some place else to put those idiots? They're giving me a headache."

"That's the doc," Meat replied as though this meant something to Donovan.

"So? Did he give you a brain transplant or something?"

Meat scowled. "He's a kid's doctor."

"Well, that explains the smiley faces on his pink tie."

"You're in rare form tonight," Nick said. "Something got you uptight?"

"No," Donovan lied, thinking of Savannah and what he would say to her when he went by her place in the morning.

"You should tell him," Meat said to Nick, nodding his head toward Donovan.

"Tell me what?" Donovan demanded, frowning.

"I guess I should have told you about this sooner." Nick shot a sideways look at Donovan. "Jesus, your timing has always stunk, you know that?"

"Yeah, yeah. Get to the point."

Nick scratched his chin and stared at the bottles behind the bar. "I wondered if you deserved to know. It's past time that this all ended. She deserves some happiness, after all. What have you ever done but been a mule-headed jackass?" he asked, swinging his gaze back to Donovan. "Who could ever get through to you once your mind was set?"

Donovan swiveled slowly on his stool. "What the hell are you talking about?"

"Savannah, you moron. She deserved a lot better than you dished out."

Donovan's hand tightened on his glass. "What happened between Savannah and me was none of your damn concern."

"Remember the swipe you took at me when you saw her leaning her head on my shoulder that day at basic? I was your best friend. We'd known each other for what, fifteen years at that point? Christ, you were a jealous son of a bitch."

"Yeah, well, I was a lot of things back then. Times change."

"And people?"

Donovan shrugged. "I guess so."

"Sometimes you have to let go of your pride to get what you want. You were never able to do that. You always protected yourself, never let your guard down. I don't think you've changed."

Donovan knew he had changed. Whether he wanted to or not, time had forced something on him. He had lived in a bubble for so long, he doubted he could ever have seen himself clearly if not for the accident and all the months he'd had nothing to do but search his own soul.

"So I was an asshole, is that what you're saying?"

A reluctant grin tugged on Nick's lips. "That's what I'm saying."

"Why do you care whether I'm a Boy Scout or not?"

"Despite popular consensus, I do give a shit about what happens to you. It was messed up, what happened to your arm. You were the best quarterback in the league."

Hearing his career spoken about in the past tense no longer stung the way it used to. "If an injury didn't take me down, age would have."

"It was a good run for a while there."

Meat nudged Nick in the arm. "So tell him already."

Nick scowled. "I'm getting there."

"Could ya hurry? I'm getting old."

With a glare at Meat, Nick turned to face Donovan. "Keep in mind that I doubted the depth of your redemption." Nick clamped a hand on the back of Donovan's neck, turned his head toward the group in the corner, and pointed at the guy in the pink tie. "Tomorrow that dude is getting married."

Donovan jerked his head away. "Wanna tell me something I don't know?"

"He's marrying Savannah."

Savannah leaned her head against the post on the back porch steps and took a deep breath.

Though her new guests were wonderful, especially the Newsomes, an elderly couple from New York who were celebrating their fiftieth wedding anniversary, the day had not been without its glitches.

Janette had never shown up. Her mother had called and told Savannah that Janette had been out all night and hadn't come home until dinnertime, and then only to climb into bed. She had been with some football player.

Mrs. Carlton hadn't mentioned the football player's name, but Savannah knew. She had seen similar gossip in the newspapers about Donovan, photographers shooting him with one gorgeous woman after the next.

It was ridiculous. She had no feelings left for Donovan, and yet her heart hurt. Perhaps it was only because she knew Janette and would have to see her every day.

Savannah sank down onto the step, absently petting Sadie. The brown Lab laid its head in her lap and rubbed her nose against Savannah's hand, looking for some loving.

She had bought Sadie when Reese was five, after Oreo, Savannah's black-and-white Maltese, had died. Donovan had bought Oreo for Savannah for her Sweet Sixteen, which fell three months after her father had died of a sudden heart attack and the weight of the world had felt as though it would suffocate her.

Oreo had been such a comfort to her. Perhaps it was then that she knew she loved Donovan. For so many years he had been her friend, her confidant. It seemed only natural to love him.

Savannah chided herself for her wandering thoughts and wondered if Jake was enjoying his party. He was such an endearing stick-in-the-mud, more prudish than most women, which was one of the things she had most liked about him. With Jake, she would never have to worry about other women. Not as she did with Donovan.

Savannah smiled as she remembered her bachelorette party a week earlier. The obligatory male stripper in his cop uniform had shown up to dance for her, but the fun had been watching her aunt blush and fuss when Savannah had turned the policeman on her. Within ten minutes, her normally sedate aunt had a fistful of dollars in her hand and was swinging a pair of handcuffs in the air.

Sadie's head suddenly jerked up, her ears alert and a low growl rumbling up her throat.

"What's the matter, girl?" Savannah heard the snap of a

twig, and Sadie jumped to her feet in a defensive stance.

"Who is it?" Savannah called out. "Who's there?"

A body moved out from a copse of trees, the face in shadows as the moon slid behind a drifting cloud only to reappear a moment later to illuminate the ground and surroundings.

And person.

"Hello, Savvy."

No one before or since Donovan had called her Savvy. He owned the nickname.

"What are you doing here?"

"That's how you greet an old friend?" he asked in that slow, seductive drawl she had always found so entrancing.

"I have the right. You're on my property." And far too close for her peace of mind as he moved to stand at the bottom of the steps.

The years had done nothing to mar his handsomeness. If anything, he was even more attractive. His features had sharpened, the leanness accentuating his rugged jaw and defining his cheekbones.

His penetrating blue eyes still had the ability to look through a person and see what was inside, as he seemed to be doing as he watched her.

"God, you're still beautiful," he said, coming up a step, forcing Savannah to move back in a subconscious gesture, catching herself before she took another step.

She folded her arms across her chest, hating the ache just seeing him caused. "What do you want, Donovan?"

"I've come to give the bride a kiss before her wedding."

So he knew. All the better. "Have you been drinking?" She could smell no alcohol—only the cologne he wore, a woodsy fragrance that slid over her as softly as the night.

He shrugged. "I had a few drinks with Meat."

Only his old football pals still called Herschel by that nickname. He now heard a new name far more often: Daddy. Herschel had five rambunctious children that he adored and who adored him.

Had Donovan run across Jake at the strip club? Is that how he had found out about her getting married, or had Herschel told him? Jake had heard some of her story about Donovan, but he didn't know the half of it.

Donovan moved to the next step, propping one foot up to rest next to hers. Lizard-skin boots adorned his feet and a Stetson was tipped back on his head, a frame for his dark, shoulder-length hair. Savannah tried to ignore the lean, muscular body in between those boots and that hat.

"Should I assume you've lost your way?" she asked, acutely aware of how close he was, how his leg lightly brushed hers.

"Nope," he replied. "In fact, I think I've finally found my way."

"How terribly prophetic you've gotten with age."

"How terribly bitter you've gotten."

Anger welled up inside her. "If you'll excuse me, I have a busy day tomorrow." She turned to go, but his words stopped her cold.

"I've missed you."

Slowly, Savannah faced him, ready to blister his ears but

reining herself in at the last moment. "I could tell. All these years you've been pining away for me, dating one super-model after the next because a case of amnesia made you forget I exist."

"Sarcasm was never your strong suit, and not very pretty."

"Forgive me if I don't care. Good night, Donovan." Savannah intended to make a grand exit and nurse her wounds with a half gallon of Ben & Jerry's Cherry Garcia ice cream, but his hand clamped around her wrist, bringing her to a sudden halt.

The next thing she knew, she was in Donovan's arms, held unrelentingly against his chest, enveloped in his scent and his heat, no words spoken as his mouth trapped hers in a breath-stealing kiss.

Her head swam. It had been so long, too long, a voice whispered. It all came back in a rush of emotions: all the love she had once felt for him, and the fun they'd had, the laughter, the tears, the ups and downs. The passion. A single kiss had the power to steal her will and bring her back to a time when everything had been good and strong and right.

Her arms rose and twined around his neck as his mouth slanted over hers, his tongue tasting her, his hands sliding down her side to nip at her waist before easing over her backside, pulling her tighter against him, letting her feel the arousal between his legs.

She remembered all the steamy nights they had spent making love, how he could bring her to a shuddering or-gasm with the simplest effort, how he would climb between her legs and hook them over his arms and stroke inside her, looking into her eyes and kissing her endlessly.

She had loved the intimacy between them, feeling as though she would never get that close to another human being, and she had believed their world would never change. But it had all been a dream that had evaporated.

Recovering her senses, Savannah pushed against Donovan's chest, her breathing heavy as she looked up at him, waiting for the outrage to pour from her, but feeling only a hollow ache.

"Let go of me," she said with surprising steadiness. Donovan hesitated, but then opened his arms. Only the wall at her back kept her from buckling. "I don't know what you're out to prove, but you won't use me to do it. I'd like you to leave my property and not return."

"I don't think that's at all what you want."

"You don't know me anymore."

"But I do. It's still there; you felt it. You just won't admit it."

"Go." She pointed. "Leave now and it will be forgotten."

"I don't want to forget. I've done that for too long. I want to talk to you."

Savannah's short laugh was tinged with bitterness. "Now you want to talk? Eight years ago you didn't. You ordered me out of your life."

"I was young and hardheaded, and too busy to listen. I've forgiven you for what happened. I don't want it to be like this forever. Not for us."

Savannah couldn't believe what she was hearing. "You've

forgiven *me?* You're unbelievable! I never did anything that required forgiveness." She shook her head. "You haven't changed, Donovan. You're still the same bullheaded, king-of-the-hill know-it-all. And you know what? I haven't forgiven *you.*" She spun around and yanked open the back door, her body rigid with indignation and banked passion.

The screen door had just banged shut when the hinges whined. She whirled around to find Donovan in the doorway, looking huge and menacing.

"I said get——" The rest of the sentence was cut off as she was hauled off her feet and thrown over his shoulder, caveman style. "Put me down!"

His lizard-skin boot kicked open the screen door, his grip sure as he carted her across the back porch and down the six steps that led to the barn and the orchard.

The night closed in around them as Donovan's determined stride carried her down the graveled driveway. Without losing a beat, he pulled open his car's door and tossed her in the passenger seat.

As Donovan dropped into the driver's seat and backed out of the driveway, she demanded, "Stop right now." When he didn't, she panicked. "Where do you think you're taking me?"

"Somewhere we can talk." Turning his head, he added pointedly, "Somewhere you can't run away."

"You'd better think of another plan. I'm getting married tomorrow."

He just kept on driving, his razor-sharp headlights the only illumination on the dark back road, the woods speeding by on the left and right looking oddly sinister.

Savannah tried to calm herself and think rationally. "You don't really believe this will solve anything?"

"We weren't solving anything your way."

"And you think this is the way to go about it? By kidnapping me?"

He smiled at her. "Yup."

Chapter three

Savannah had the strongest desire to stomp her feet. How dare he! He had no right to think he could just walk in after all this time and expect her to welcome him with open arms.

"Why don't you just drop me off here? Janette lives only a few miles away. I'm sure she'd appreciate your caveman antics far more."

He had the good sense to look shamefaced. "You heard about that, did you?"

"She's twenty-two, you old lech."

"Need I remind you that I'm only thirty?"

Savannah didn't care. And it didn't help that he was a stunning thirty, to boot. Did the man never age?

"You kept her from her job."

"I didn't even know she was there, so how could I have kept her from anything?"

"That's not surprising. You always did care for only yourself."

"That's not true and you know it." A wicked half-grin

turned up his lips as he shot a glance at her. "You're jealous."

"Hah!" Oh, she was certainly full of great comebacks.

"This is priceless." He shook his head, his smile intact. "Nothing happened with her."

"I really don't care. All I care about are my guests, who very nearly arrived to dirty rooms."

"That's right. You turned your parents' place into a B & B, and a very successful one, from what I've heard."

She would appeal to his sense of decency—her business would be in jeopardy if she wasn't there to oversee things. He didn't need to know her aunt and brother were in place to take over for her during her two-week honeymoon.

"So certainly you must see that I have to get back to my guests?"

A dimple appeared in his cheek. He was laughing at her. "Don't think to pull the wool over my eyes; I know you too well. Just sit tight. We'll be there in a few minutes."

"Where?"

He wouldn't answer, damn him. She surveyed him from her captive's seat, wondering if a full-blown temper tantrum would get him to stop. She doubted it. She knew what a pigheaded mule he could be when he set his mind to something.

Fine, she would go with the flow. Fighting would only get him hovering over her even more. He had something to say, so she would let him say it and be done.

His Aston Martin Vanquish turned down a heavily wooded dirt road that sparked a memory in her, a feeling that she had traveled this way a long time ago.

He slid an unreadable look her way. The woods suddenly opened up to a wide clearing, and Savannah saw the big old plantation house in the distance, sitting on the rim of Crawfish Lake.

How could she have forgotten this place? They had spent so many lazy afternoons and warm summer nights here, talking, laughing. Making love when it had verged on the forbidden because of their age.

"Remember?"

Words deserted her and her heart beat in slow, thick strokes, a heavy lump in her throat.

The Vanquish came to a purring stop at the front door of Donovan's grandparents' old home, Magnolia Hills. His grandfather had died eleven years earlier, his grandmother shortly thereafter—from a broken heart, Donovan's mother had said at the funeral.

Donovan's grandparents had shared a special bond, sixty-one years of marriage. It was practically unheard of. Savannah realized now why the Newsomes, her elderly couple who were visiting for the week, had held such a fascination for her. They had reminded her of Grandma and Grandpa Jerricho.

Donovan came around and opened the car door for her, putting his hand out. Hesitantly, Savannah took it and stepped around him to look up at the house. At the sight of the old-fashioned porch that wrapped around the front and sides of the house, time turned back for her.

She could picture the Hills as it was the last time she had been here, whitewashed and gleaming in the late-day sun as she sat in one of the many rocking chairs with Grandma Jerricho sipping a cold, sweet lemonade that never failed to take the edge off the Mississippi humidity.

She walked to the porch railing, the full moon reflecting on the water and over the eaves like white gold.

"How many times did I kiss you in this very spot?" Donovan asked in a low, deep tone that sent shivers down her arms.

"Don't," she said as he pulled her into his embrace, the ghosts of the past wrapping around her, taking her back to a time when life had been simple and she had loved him with a young girl's heart. How naive she had been. How foolish.

Savannah fought not to close her eyes and lean into his palm as he cupped her face, his eyes sensuous and intense.

She wet her lips and swallowed the dryness in her throat. "You said you had something to say to me. Please say it so that we can get this over with."

"Are you that eager to get back to your fiancé?"

With a guilty start, Savannah realized she had not thought about Jake since she'd spotted Donovan walking toward her. And worse, Jake hadn't been on her mind half as much as Donovan since his homecoming.

"I'm worried about my daughter," she said.

"Reese," he said, surprising her.

"Yes."

"Short for Clarisse, right?"

Savannah nodded.

"You told me if you ever had a girl, you would name her Clarisse. Michael if you had a boy."

"That was a long time ago."

"Some things you don't forget." The poignancy in his voice tugged at Savannah's heart. "So why didn't you marry Reese's father? And do you still want that little boy?"

Savannah had tucked away the dream of having another child. Reese's birth had been emotional, and the prospects of raising her alone frightening.

Savannah had been barely twenty years old, and though her family had always been there for her, she had felt utterly alone.

She slid out of Donovan's embrace and walked to the corner of the porch, an overhang of honeysuckle scenting the air and making wispy patterns on the glassy surface of the water. "Why didn't you ever marry?" she asked instead of answering his question.

She felt him as he moved to stand behind her, his closeness like a caress. "I've only been in love once and that didn't work out."

Was he talking about her, or another woman? And did she really want to know?

Savannah turned to face him, suddenly desperate to leave, to get as far away from him as possible before . . .

She shut out the thought. Nothing was going to happen. Tomorrow she would be a married woman. She loved Jake. Perhaps her feelings for him weren't quite the same as they had been for Donovan, but he was a good, solid man and he loved Reese. He would make a wonderful father. Far better than Reese's real father.

"This is not right. Surely you see that," she said.

"Do you hate me that much?"

"I don't hate you at all. I feel nothing."

"Nothing?" he murmured, moving closer to her, his heat wrapping around her. "Are you sure about that?"

Savannah forced herself to meet his gaze. "Whatever I felt for you was a long time ago. It's dead and buried now. You saw to that."

He sighed and glanced down. "Yeah." He shook his head. "I don't know what to say. There was so much happening then. I wasn't sure of myself, let alone the two of us."

"But you were sure of what I had done, weren't you?"

"At the time, I thought so. It all seemed so clear."

"And is it still that clear to you now?"

"If you're asking if I still think you cheated on me, the answer is no. I didn't want to believe it even then." He glanced out at a spot beyond her shoulder. "It's just that when I saw you in my best friend's arms, I went crazy. I could barely stand a guy looking at you, let alone touching you. I know that was my own insecurity, but I was still a kid in a lot of ways. A kid with a two-million-dollar contract and way too much hype." His gaze slid back to her. "I came back to talk to you then, you know."

She frowned. "When?"

"About two months after we separated, once I had gotten up the courage to face you. I had finally talked with Kyle and I knew the whole story. I was prepared for you to throw grenades at my head."

Kyle Henton had been one of Donovan's closest friends

since grammar school, and after Donovan had accused them of cheating, Savannah had never seen Kyle again.

"Talked? I heard you beat each other senseless."

He grinned. "Well, we did. But after we had bloodied each other up, we talked. He told me nothing happened, that whatever I thought had gone on was only in my mind. But I had seen a pattern, or what I thought was one. The way you began to stay out after work and didn't want . . ." He stopped.

"Want?" Savannah said, trying to rein in her rising anger at what she was hearing. Because Kyle had said nothing happened, that resolved everything in Donovan's mind. He hadn't trusted or loved her enough to ask *her* directly, to believe in what she would say.

He shrugged, but his eyes were hot as he looked down at her. "You didn't seem to want sex."

Fury shot up Savannah's spine. She tried to wrest herself free of his hold, but he wouldn't release her. "You're incredible. Because I worked late and was tired, you believed I was cheating on you?"

He took hold of both her arms, forcing her to face him fully. "I was a stupid kid, Savannah. I loved you so much. I would have given up everything for you, and that scared the shit out of me. We had always been so hot and heavy. We couldn't get enough of each other.

"God," he said with a heartfelt ache in his voice, "I remember all those nights we made love, the way you would slide over me, your body so soft and warm, your mouth hungry against my skin . . . your hands pumping me. We'd do it in the shower, on the kitchen floor, the hallway, the living room. I remember that time at school when we pushed the emergency stop and did it in the elevator. We just . . ."

He shook his head. "I don't know. But when it stopped, I thought you didn't want me anymore and it ate me up inside. Maybe I was just looking for an excuse when I found you and Kyle together."

Kyle had become as much her friend as Donovan's, perhaps closer to her as Donovan got more and more famous, too busy for his childhood friends. And for her.

She had felt shut out, and he had not been the only one who was jealous. She'd had to watch for years as first the high school cheerleaders and then the buxom college cheerleaders fawned all over him, flirting with him.

How could she compete with such women? She was just a skinny, unworldly Southern girl, a memory of a life he wanted to leave behind. And all those emotions and fears came to a head the day that Donovan found her in Kyle's embrace.

She could understand why he had been angry. Had she found him in another woman's embrace, she would have felt the same. But the way he closed her out, as though she had never meant anything to him—*that* she could not forget. Or forgive.

"Let me go." She tried to move around him, but he remained firm.

"I let you go once and it was the biggest mistake of my life. I'm not giving up so easily this time."

Without warning, he leaned down and kissed her, and Savannah felt her body instantly respond, just as she had when they were randy college students, unable to keep their hands off each other.

Her good sense told her to stop, but she couldn't. Her brain wouldn't slow down to wonder about what she was doing or feeling; she just wanted it to go on.

Her hands slid up his soft cotton shirt and twined unconsciously in his hair, still silky and long.

The newspapers had labeled him one of the top ten most eligible bachelors, a model with a helmet and cleats, an Adonis for that hair and his spectacular physique.

He was, but it had been the boy who lived inside the famous football hero that she had loved.

He pressed into her, his arousal a hard, hot length against her belly, and she couldn't seem to stop herself from moving against him, from reveling in the low moan that rumbled up his throat and the way his hands tensed against her sides, gripping and releasing, testing her flesh.

He pushed her back against the railing, lifting her to sit on the edge, her legs spread around his hips, her pelvis ground against his.

He took hold of her hair and tugged her head back, his mouth moving along her neck, lavishing kisses on every piece of skin, making her shiver.

His lips trailed down the V of her blouse, a few small buttons the only thing keeping them from going too far. But it had gone too far already.

Savannah bit her lip as Donovan's big, warm hand settled on her breast, cupping, massaging, lightly teasing her nipple, which pressed insistently against the thin, lacy cup of her bra.

She was a grown, responsible woman with a child and a fiancé, but her mind balked at acting that way now. She had been responsible for so many years.

Her hand instinctively moved down the waistband of Donovan's jeans, sliding over his erection, his mouth slanting over hers with urgency.

He groaned and lifted her off the railing, her feet dangling inches from the ground as he cupped the back of her head and continued to kiss her as he moved to the front door.

Savannah barely heard the screech of the old hinges as he carried her over the threshold and into the house.

It brought her back to the time when the house was alive with family and friends, and the days of Mississippi State and future disasters were yet to be seen. They had still been innocent and free.

The back of her legs brushed against the sofa, covered with a white sheet, which Donovan yanked off before he laid her down.

Her arms were still looped around his neck, pulling him down with her and over her, his weight heavy but welcomed.

She felt like a virginal teenager as he shifted to the side so that he could move his hand to the top of her blouse, the first button sliding like butter through the hole, the second giving way just as easily.

At the third, Savannah covered his hand with hers, her mind fighting to regain some measure of common sense, though her body protested every step of the way.

She couldn't allow Donovan to just walk back into her

life and turn it upside down. He had done that in college and she had thought she would never recover. She could not risk her entire future—again—on a man who would most likely walk out on her. She needed stability. A home.

Happiness.

She deserved it now. And not only for herself, but also for her daughter.

"Stop."

"Just give me tonight, Savannah," he begged as his fingers feathered over a nipple, making her breath catch in her throat.

"Why?" she demanded, struggling to her elbows. "So you can come back and ruin my life again?"

"No." He brushed a piece of hair from her face. "So I can have one last memory with you, if this is all I'll ever have. We both need to get this out of our system. There's still something between us, no matter how much you believe you hate me. I think this moment says differently."

"This moment says I temporarily lost my mind. Nothing more." She pushed at his shoulders and fought to sit up, her head swimming from his kisses.

His hand slid firmly up her spine and under the hair at the back of her neck, gently sifting the long strands through his fingers, making goose bumps rise on her arms. "Doesn't it mean anything to you that I still have feelings for you?"

Instead of his words being a salve to her heart, all they did was cause pain. "No," she bit out, rising to her feet and turning to face him. "Not now. Not all these years later."

Her body quaked with anger and suppressed desire. "God, you think a kiss and a smile will make everything better? You waltz back into my life when you feel like it and think I'll stop everything for you? Well, I won't, Donovan. Do you understand? I won't. Tomorrow I *will* be Mrs. Jake Marshall—and you *will* be forgotten."

CHAPTER FOUR

*T*he slow clapping cut Savannah's dramatic exit short. She whirled around to see Donovan leaning back against the armrest of the sofa, his body negligently draped across it, his jacket having been divested somewhere along the way, exposing his crisp white shirt and the hard plane of muscle beneath.

"That was a gifted performance of outrage. Oscar-worthy, in fact."

Savannah fisted her hands at her sides, struggling to keep from throwing something at him. "You think this is funny? You could be arrested for kidnapping."

"Are you going to press charges, Savvy?"

"Don't call me that."

"Bother you?"

More than he knew. "I'm getting married, Donovan. Do you understand? This is not a game."

Jake had been there for her when Reese had nearly died from a virulent strain of the flu. He had stayed with her every step of the way.

During that long night, Savannah had realized she had feelings for him. Maybe those feelings were more of gratitude than love at first, but Jake had become an anchor for her, a safe harbor, and she had needed that.

"Guess now you'll live safely behind your picket fence, planting your garden and taking stray cats into your perfect life."

His assessment hurt and angered her. "That's right. So why don't you let me get back to it?"

His hands reached up to bracket her face. "Because, Savannah, I still love you."

Emotions churned wildly inside her, feelings and needs that she had believed exorcised long, long ago. She pulled back. "You don't mean it."

"I do. The moment I saw you, I knew I had made a mistake in pushing you out of my life. But when I found out you were pregnant . . ." He shrugged and glanced away. "I figured you had moved on. I was so damn sure I was over you. But I wasn't." His gaze slid back to her. "I'm not. I know my timing isn't good—"

"Isn't good?" A bubble of irrational laughter rose up in Savannah. "That's an understatement. Your timing stinks."

She dropped down into a chair and gripped one hand in the other to keep them steady. She would not fall apart now.

"So what do we do now?" he asked as silence descended. "Do we pretend this never happened? That I never said what I said? Should we go so far as to believe that we were simply a figment of the other's imagination and that what we shared was just a dream?"

Savannah leaned her head into her hands. "I don't know."

Donovan kneeled before her, taking her wrists into his hands. "Look at me."

Savannah hesitated, then glanced up.

"Stay with me tonight. One night, Savannah. I can have you back in the morning before anyone knows you're gone. All I want is this little bit of time with you. A few hours."

"So you just want to have sex with me, is that what you're saying?"

"I'm saying that I want to be with you. I came home for you, Savannah."

Savannah wanted to put her hands over her ears. "You came home because your illustrious career abruptly ended. You're going through a crisis, a trial of faith. Perhaps you've even found yourself. But none of that matters. It's too late, Donovan. There is no going back."

Slowly, he rose to his feet and Savannah knew her barb had struck home. It should feel good, unleashing all that anger she had pent up, but it only made her feel small and petty.

He turned from her and went to stand in front of the bay window overlooking the lake.

"I guess I deserved that." His voice was edged with hurt and it pained Savannah to hear it, but she could not own his hurt. She had enough of her own.

He shifted to face her and sat on the windowsill. "Is Reese my daughter?"

His question hit her like a bucket of ice water.

She stared at him as numbness settled over her body. "I don't understand what you're talking about."

"Yes, you do. Your lack of an answer and the look on your face tell me everything. Shame on me, right? Deep down, I think I knew that you could never cheat on me. You loved me too much." He paused. "I'm pretty sure you still do."

Savannah sprang up out of her chair and headed for the door, desperation chasing at her heels. As her fingers wrapped around the doorknob, Donovan's hand snaked around her upper arm, whipping her around before pinning her up against the door.

"Not so fast. You owe me an explanation."

"I owe you nothing."

"We'll see what the courts have to say."

Savannah's heart missed a beat. "You'd take me to court?"

"Do you think I won't? You've kept my child from me. You had no right."

"I had every right!" Savannah cried, fear constricting her chest into a painful knot. "You didn't want to hear anything I had to say. God forbid something should derail your football career. How many times did I hear you say that kids were a hindrance, that they would only get in the way? In the way of what, Donovan? Your fame? Your ego? Or just in the way of being free of me?"

"That's bullshit and you know it."

Savannah laughed bitterly, a single tear coursing down her face, which she swiped at. "Is it? Think back. Remember how absorbed you were in everything and everyone but me. I went to Kyle because I needed someone to talk to, someone who would listen. I almost *wanted* him to come on to me, because I was so hurt and angry at you. I wanted to get you back for not caring. But when a moment presented it-self, I couldn't do it. I couldn't hurt you or Kyle. You both meant too much to me."

"Savannah—"

"You nearly killed me, Donovan. There were days when I thought I couldn't live without you. But when I almost miscarried Reese, I knew I had to pull myself together. I couldn't lose the last thing that I had of you. I needed her. And she needed me."

"She needed me too, Savannah."

"Oh, please. You were with another woman by then. Re-member Cara Hunter, the supermodel? I certainly do. I had to see the two of you in every magazine for months."

"She was a friend."

"Is that what they're calling it these days?"

"I was hurt."

"Well, sorry, I guess I should have shoved my own pain down and only thought of yours. I meant so much to you, after all."

"I never wanted any of this to happen."

"But it did. You closed me out and I couldn't bear to have you in my life as a part-time father to Reese, to have you come and go. I didn't want a world of weekend visitations and every other holiday and birthdays. I didn't want you to decide one day that you didn't want Reese, either. I couldn't bear it if she was hurt."

"You think that little of me, do you?"

Tears rolled down Savannah's cheeks in earnest even though she had closed her eyes to try to staunch the flow. "I needed you gone. Forgotten. That was the only way I could manage every day." She opened her eyes and looked up at him. "You can't take her away from me. I won't let you."

His grip eased on her shoulders. "I'd never take her away, Savvy. That's not what I want." He dropped his hands and stepped back. "Christ, I don't even know if I could have been a good father to her. You're right, I was self-absorbed. I didn't realize it until my injury forced me to take stock of my life. Three months of being laid up kicks your ass right into a good bout of self-examination. It's not pretty to look at the failures of your life, to realize you took the wrong road." He gently wiped a tear from her cheek. "But I'm glad I was forced to realize that. If it hadn't, I wouldn't be here with you."

"Please, Donovan—"

"Do you love him, Savannah? Is he really what you want?"

At that moment, Savannah didn't know what she wanted. She was so confused, and Donovan was too close, too dangerous to her senses.

Her feelings for him had never truly died. They had simply lain dormant, buried as best as she could manage. Just seeing him had immediately brought those feelings to the surface, and only the pain of his previous defection kept them from spilling over.

"Yes," she murmured in a tear-laden voice, "I love Jake." But never the way she had loved Donovan. And Jake deserved a woman who would love him completely, whose heart would not always belong to another man.

But she could love Jake the way he deserved, given time. She would not allow Donovan's vows of renewed devotion make her doubt herself.

"Will you at least let me see Reese?" he asked, looking suddenly tired and defeated.

"Of course." She couldn't deny him any longer, and Reese deserved the truth. "About what I said earlier . . ."

"It's water under the bridge now. What's done is done."

He turned from her and walked away. Savannah nearly reached for him, her heart aching over what she had done.

He didn't deserve this, no matter what had happened between them. But back when it was all happening, she hadn't seen it that way.

For weeks after Reese was born, she had told herself daily that she would call Donovan, that he should know about his daughter, and if he told her to get lost, then she would have her answer and be free of any guilt.

But one day had turned into another. Weeks became months. Months melted into years. The time never seemed right. Then she simply blanked out that phase of her life and continued on as though she had never known Donovan Jerricho.

"So what do we do now?" she asked softly.

"I guess I take you home. That's what you want, isn't it?"

She had thought so—but now she wasn't so sure. Her heart felt as though it was dissolving into little pieces.

"Yes," she answered, knowing she was doing the right thing. She faced the door and turned the knob, the low keen of the hinges the only sound in the silence.

Like a polite stranger, Donovan took her by the elbow and they walked in silence to his car, a low-slung, gleaming machine that seemed out of place amid the tall grass and chirp of crickets.

He opened the passenger-side door for her and waited for her to get in. But something in Savannah made her stop, then turn, and take Donovan's face between her palms and bring his lips down to hers in a slow, sensual kiss that had her clinging to him in the sultry night air.

"Savannah . . ."

"Don't say anything. Please, Donovan—just take me back inside."

CHAPTER FIVE

*W*ithout a word, he did as she asked, his movements fluid as he lifted her into his arms, kicking the car door shut with his booted foot and carrying her back up the porch steps and over the threshold into the house, like a man carrying his wife.

If he closed the front door, she didn't hear it. His mouth had returned to hers and he kissed her with such passion it took her breath away.

Savannah felt reckless and frantic for him. She needed this time with him, needed to get him out of her system once and for all, she told herself as he carried her down a long hall.

She knew this spot. It was his old bedroom, and it was just as she remembered it. In the corner sat the big mahogany bed, with its carved headboard and posts, which supported an extralarge mattress to fit his footballer's frame.

At times during high school Donovan had hoisted her in through the window and they had lain in his bed, touching and kissing.

She had been a good and proper Southern girl then and had never let it go too far. But he had introduced her to pleasure without intercourse, when simply having his mouth on her nipples could bring her to orgasm.

She hadn't thought anything could be better—then he had shown her all the joy she could derive from having his hand between her legs.

And when she turned eighteen, she finally discovered the ecstasy of having his big, solid body between her thighs; knew the true meaning of being one.

She had craved that connection between them like some wanton, sex-starved woman. He would just laugh and snatch her up in his arms, always prepared to give her what she wanted—just as he did now as he eased down on top of her, his fingers entwining with hers, spreading her arms wide then moving them over her head as he pressed against her, his arousal hot and hard and tempting.

His mouth moved along her jaw, his warm, moist breath fanning over her skin, making her shiver as he kissed and licked her neck, her collarbone, the naked flesh between her breasts.

Savannah arched up as he nosed aside the material of her blouse and closed his mouth over her nipple through the thin material of her bra. She groaned and pressed up against him, her body twisting under his, wanting more.

He manacled both her wrists in one of his hands above her head, keeping her immobile as his free hand traveled down her side, gently squeezing her waist before pulling her blouse free of her jeans, the warmth of his palm settling over her stomach, massaging in slow circles, making her nearly crazy with desire.

She wanted him to undo the button and ease down the zipper. She wanted his hands down there, his finger slipping between her moist folds. She was so ready, so wet and throbbing. The tension was almost too much to bear.

She freed one of her hands and gripped his arm, her fingers digging into the enormous band of muscle that had made him such a dynamo on the playing field. That arm had been pure gold once.

She raised his hand to her mouth and kissed it, momentarily stilling him as he watched her kiss each of his fingers, gently rolling up his shirtsleeve to reveal the jagged scars left from two surgeries to repair a break that would never properly heal and that would keep him from playing the game he had loved so much.

Her lips softly feathered over the wound, her eyes never leaving his as her tongue lightly lapped at the injury.

She hurt so deeply for him. He may have hurt her worse than anything she could have imagined, but no matter what he had done, he did not deserve such a blow.

She wanted to ask him what he would do now that he could no longer play ball, if he had other dreams and aspirations, but a husky growl rumbled up his throat, giving her only a moment's warning before his mouth came down over hers in a demanding kiss that took her breath away.

The heat rising from his body was heady and intoxicating. A languorous warmth coursed up her arms and over her chest before sinking lower, his heat becoming part of her as a throbbing ache built at the juncture of her thighs.

He took hold of her hand and moved it up his inner thigh, her fingers brushing the hardness centered there. She ached for the feel of him inside her, to know if it was as good as her memory.

Her body thrummed as her left hand swept against his rigid length. She heard his sharp intake of breath and felt satisfaction.

Sweet Mary, he was virile—a heavenly made male in the prime of his life, but with a tempered maturity that was all the more mesmerizing.

She massaged his erection through his jeans, feeling him swell. Air hissed through his teeth as she cupped his balls and scratched lightly with her nails.

When she looked up at his face, she saw passion raging almost out of control. He rolled to his back and urgently tugged her pants down, then dragged her across his lap, her naked thighs straddling him.

Wet heat dampened her panties. He pressed up against her, rocking his erection against her barely shielded cleft.

He cupped her breasts and she let out a low moan as his thumbs swept across the rigid peaks, making her mindless with desire as he flicked and rubbed and rolled her nipples between his fingers. Her inner lips clenched, a throbbing welling deep inside her.

His hands moved to the edge of her blouse, and without a word, he ripped every button from the silky material, wrenching the breath from her lungs. Her body quivered with rising anticipation.

Savannah gyrated against him, pleasure flushing her skin, her scent rising hot and musky between them.

She arched against his hands on her breasts, wanting his mouth on her.

He pulled her forward and his tongue slid out and flicked one nipple. She jolted as he teased the peak, moistening it, circling, lapping, her body quickening with each passing second.

He moved to her other nipple to lavish it with the same attention he had shown the first, before cupping her breasts and pushing them together, drawing one sensitive nub deep into his mouth and then moving to the other to offer it the same attention.

Savannah moaned his name, wild with desire. All she could do was hold on to his shoulders and revel in the friction her own movement created between their bodies.

"Yes," she breathed as he continued to tug on her nipple while his free hand skimmed up her calf, pausing to stroke the tender flesh behind her knee before resuming his journey along her outer thigh.

His fingers brushed the base of her spine, leaving a path of prickling skin to tantalize her before drifting around to the front and sliding his hand down the front of her cotton panties.

The first touch of his finger against her clitoris made Savannah cry out with pleasure; the erect nub was hot and exquisitely sensitive, pouring bliss through her veins. His mouth created wet paths between her breasts as he massaged her.

"Please," she moaned as his finger slowed to torturous circles. She wanted him to stroke her faster, but he wanted to torment her, to tease.

Each time she felt on the brink of heaven, it was as if he knew and would purposely ease back, kiss around her nipple, lick beneath her breast, make one taunting sweep with his tongue across the aching tip. Then he would start again, building the tension, the need, until Savannah thought she would disintegrate.

She tore urgently at the buttons of his shirt, needing to lay her hands against his hard flesh, pressing against the muscles that bunched and flexed with every move he made.

"Donovan!"

"Whatever you want," he murmured in a passion-roughened voice, as his mouth latched onto her nipple and his finger resumed the torture on her throbbing core, flicking back and forth so that she was bucking and writhing, dying inside for that sweet release she knew he could give her, until her back arched, her entire body tensing, lightning gathering deep inside her and spiraling downward as her first convulsion pulsed through her, followed by a second and a third and a fourth as Donovan made light circles before his finger slid down to her opening to sweep inside her. Savannah moaned at the sensation, each contraction clutching him.

He began to pump and she closed her eyes, the intoxication stirring once more. She wriggled, yearning for him to go deeper, and heard his harsh groan.

Savannah ground her hips against him. He grabbed hold

of her wrists, pinioning them at her sides as he stared into her eyes, looking fierce and tender.

With a growl, he leaned forward and kissed her nipple, the tip so incredibly sensitive from all the attention he had given it that her inner lips contracted one more time.

With a deep, almost desperate breath, he leaned back against the pillows and gently righted the blouse that his big hands had ripped down the middle, an expression on his face that told her that he wanted to talk, not take advantage of her vulnerability.

But talking was the last thing she wanted. She didn't want to be reasonable or sensible or drift back to that place of pretense.

She wanted to feel his hands on her, flesh against flesh, with no barriers. She had missed him so much, longed for him to ease the ache in her heart as well as her body.

She reached out to run a finger down the deep V of his half-open shirt, smiling at the way his gaze followed her every move.

Something caught her eye then and she eased back the right side of his shirt, shocked to see a small, perfectly drawn heart positioned directly above his real heart.

She stared, not quite sure what she was seeing. The tattoo reminded her of the heart she had once etched on an old birch tree down by Sweetwater Bayou, where she and Donovan used to go to spend time alone. They had used his old pocketknife to etch the shape and then both of them had carved their initials.

"D. J. . . ." She sucked in a breath. "And S.H." Those

were the initials forever marking his skin inside the heart tattoo. She glanced up at him, confused.

"I got it done the morning before we broke up. I was going to surprise you. It seemed a romantic thing to do at the time."

Had she seen it then, she would have melted, cried on the spot that he had done such a thing while lecturing him on the potential dangers of tattooing—unclean tools and hepatitis. He had always laughed at the way she worried about him.

Savannah traced its shape with her finger, feeling the smooth, solid flesh beneath, the muscles that delineated Donovan's rock-hard upper chest and rippled down his stomach, her gaze fixed on the initials inside that heart.

All these years and he had never tried to have it removed. She knew laser procedures could have obliterated it, leaving no more than a slight discoloration on his skin. Why had he never done it?

She leaned forward and kissed his nipple, lapping gently at it until it hardened. Then she drew the pebble into her mouth as he had with her, reveling in the way his body tensed. Raising her head, she pressed her mouth to his, her tongue slipping across the taut line of his hard-won control.

With a groan, he parted his lips, and she stroked inside, wrapping her arms around his neck and pressing closer, wanting to get closer still . . . wanting him inside, to be one with him in a way she had only dreamed about for a long time.

Boldly, Savannah put her hand between them and discovered he was still erect. She unbuttoned his jeans. Her mouth still fused to his, she reached inside his boxers and found him silky and hot, flame hot. He moaned into her mouth as she began to stroke him.

He tore his mouth from hers and tipped his head back, his expression one of rapt ecstasy as her hands glided over him. He had taught her so much all those years ago, things she had not forgotten, desires long suppressed and aching for this moment.

Savannah pressed his erection against her moist cleft and began sliding back and forth. He stared at her with heavy-lidded eyes, passion turning them a dark, cobalt blue that burned with fire.

Jaw clenched, he coiled an arm around her waist and used his free hand to drag her blouse off her shoulders and throw it off the bed.

Her bra followed suit, then he leaned up and latched onto a nipple, sending a rush of sensation straight to the center of her.

She rode him faster, wanting him inside, yet she was too frantic, too wild, another thundering climax looming over the next horizon as he took possession of her mouth and toyed with her nipples.

Savannah cried into his mouth as her release spiraled through her, her entire body tensing with that sweet saturation, the pulses deep and fast.

She fell against his chest, breathing hard, his hands kneading her flesh. Only with Donovan had she ever been this sexually explosive. And still she wanted him yet again.

Savannah opened her eyes and found him staring down at her, hovering there like some Dionysian god, all dark and beautiful. He kneed her thighs apart, and she gazed up at the dark canopy above her with passion-glazed eyes, a sigh of rapture falling from her lips as his finger slid between her cleft and found her swollen nub, rubbing in circles until she was panting his name. How did he manage to excite her again so quickly? And so many times?

The thought was obliterated as he flicked her nipple with the tip of his tongue, working his magic between her thighs, bringing Savannah to the brink of ecstasy time and again.

With only their hot breath whispering in the darkness, he slid down her body and his mouth replaced his fingers. The first touch of his tongue upon the engorged pulse point made her hips buck wildly.

She tossed her head back and forth. "Donovan," she whimpered over and over.

His fingers came up and circled her nipples, but he would not touch them. Savannah thrust her breasts into his palms, and still he tortured her, so that she finally clamped her hands over his and made him touch her.

His forefingers flicked her nipples once, twice, three times before her entire body tensed, holding her on the brink for a heartbeat, before she began to convulse.

In the next breath, he slid into her, her swollen tissue clenching around him as he began to pump, her body sighing into him with each thrust.

He lifted her hips and wrapped her legs around his flanks, which brought him deep inside her. "Savannah . . ." Her name on his lips was the most glorious thing she had ever heard.

He rocked her, his thrusts growing faster, his face racked with an expression that was near to anguish, sweat glistening on his brow as he forced himself to slow, easing out of her entirely in the next moment.

A protest sprang to her lips, but then he began to massage the nub between her dewy folds with his hot, silky shaft as he sucked on her nipple.

She cried out with another orgasm, her nails digging into his back as he drove into her again, his hands gripping her buttocks, pulling her tighter against his groin as he plunged into her.

Suddenly, he snaked his arm behind her back and turned her over so that she was on her hands and knees. He grabbed hold of her hips and slid into her again, her sheath clenching his shaft as he stroked in and out of her.

He reached his hand beneath her and began massaging her clitoris, her hair a silken jumble around her face, cascading over her shoulders and skimming the sheets, her nipples peeking through the dark veil each time he pumped.

Mindless, she panted his name as he rocked inside her, until another shattering release washed over her and he finally found his own release.

He dropped down beside her and they both lay there staring up at the ceiling, trying to catch their breath while the night breeze cooled their overheated bodies.

CHAPTER SIX

Savannah lay in Donovan's bed as still as a stone, wondering if she could just fade away.

Did she have no restraint? No common decency? How could she do this to Jake when he had been nothing but good and kind to her?

Well, she had no choice. She would have to go to him and tell him the truth, and whatever he decided to do, she would live with it. She doubted he would forgive her for this and she couldn't blame him. She didn't know if she could forgive herself.

She felt Donovan's head turn on the pillow but she could not look at him. She wanted to blame him, but she was as much—or perhaps more—at fault than he was. He had agreed to take her home, had walked her to his car without further protest. She had been the one to kiss him. She had seen to her own downfall.

Savannah turned on her side, away from him. He laid a hand on her shoulder but said nothing, though she knew he wanted to.

Was he feeling any regret for his actions? Or only a sense of satisfaction that he had managed to destroy her life again? How she could have fallen so far, so fast, she had yet to sort out.

For a long time, she listened to the soft melody of a lark singing outside, waiting for the sound of Donovan's steady breathing, to tell her he had drifted off to sleep.

When he finally did, Savannah slipped from the bed and stood there in the darkened room, staring down at him. Once upon a time she would have given anything to remain like this, to stay in his arms forever.

She closed her eyes and took a deep breath, then she moved away from the bed and out the door, down the long corridor toward the front of the house.

On a chair by the front door she found Donovan's discarded jacket. Inside the right pocket, she fished out the keys to his car.

She walked down the steps and toward the Vanquish in a fog, wondering how she would explain her infidelity to the 150 guests who would be arriving that afternoon. How could she face Jake's mother and grandmother? Or his sister, whom Savannah had become such good friends with?

Like a robot, she turned the key in the ignition. The car's engine turned over with barely a sound. She flicked on the lights and spewed up stones as she sped down the long tunnel of the driveway and back out onto the road, dreading the fast-approaching morning.

Soon she was pulling into her narrow driveway, parking

the car by the same clump of bushes Donovan had, to hide the car from view.

What reason would she give her daughter when Jake called everything off? And, God, what was she going to tell her about Donovan? He was her father, after all. Savannah could no longer walk around with blinders on. She could not deny the man his daughter.

"Where the hell have you been?"

Savannah nearly jumped a foot as she neared the back steps and almost ran smack into her brother, who was coming around the side of the house. He had a strange expression on his face, and concern rifled through Savannah.

"What's happened? What's going on?"

"That's a question you have to answer. Where in the blue blazes have you been? I walked past your room a half hour ago and saw the door partially opened, but your bed looked as though you hadn't slept in it. I've been frantic, looking around here. I thought maybe you had decided to elope with old Jake."

Not even close, she thought despondently. "I was . . . out."

He crossed his arms over his chest. "Out? Where could you have been at—" he checked his watch—"five-thirty in the morning?"

Savannah closed her eyes. She had spent nearly six hours with Donovan. The morning was closing in much faster than she had thought. Marlene would be at the house at eight to do her nails and hair.

"It's a long story," she said with a sigh as she moved past her brother and up the stairs. "Can we talk about it later?"

"No. We'll talk about it now."

With her hand on the doorknob, Savannah looked over her shoulder. "You're not my father, Frank, as much as you like to act like it."

"Well, that's gratitude. I raised you after mom died, protected you, fed you, did everything I could for you, and this is what I get?"

He was right. He had always been there for her. And it was clear he had been terribly worried. "All right. Just promise me you won't get angry or do anything foolish," she added, knowing her brother's temper.

With her last bit of energy, she explained what had happened after Donovan had made his late-night appearance on her doorstep.

She tried to play down some of the evening's events, leaving out one event entirely as that was private and not for her brother's ears.

But no matter how calmly she endeavored to explain, Frank's face changed from concerned to angry to enraged.

"That lousy, motherfucking son of a bitch. I'll kill him."

Savannah came down the steps and put her hands firmly on her brother's shoulders. "Now, Frank, stop that kind of talk."

Frank looked her straight in the eyes and said, "He's dead. Mark my words."

Alarm whipped through Savannah's veins. "You, promised you wouldn't get angry."

"I lied. Give me a ten-minute head start then call the cops. They'll be scraping his carcass off the floor with a spatula."

He swung away from her and Savannah raced ahead of him to block his path. "I'm not going to let you do this."

"You're going to stop me?"

"I'm asking you to let me handle this. I'm not a little girl anymore, Frank. I know what to do."

His jaw tightened. "That bastard just decides to show up and ruin your life all over again? Well, I'm not going to let him, Savannah. Do you hear me? I couldn't bear to see you go through what you went through last time. Not again, damn it. He deserves to pay for this."

Savannah's heart lurched. Beneath his gruff exterior, her brother had a heart of gold. He had suffered right along with her when Donovan had left the first time.

Frank was such a strong man, but her father used to always say that she could make him crumble, and for a man like Frank, that was never easy.

He wore his masculinity like a badge. He did not like anything that threatened to break it down, and she had the power to do that to him.

"Frank," she said softly, "I'm stronger now—thanks to you. You have always been there for me and I will never forget that. Donovan doesn't have the power to hurt me like he once did. The first time gave me a tougher armor. And don't believe it was all him, this time. I played an active role."

She turned halfway from him and stared down the driveway, toward the spot where Donovan's car was hidden. "Perhaps I had things of my own that I wanted to say. Perhaps I needed this time with him to let him go once and for all."

"And have you let him go?"

Savannah wished with every fiber of her being that she could say yes, that she was completely and totally over Donovan, and that nothing he said or did mattered to her one way or the other.

But something inside her couldn't do it. Some speck of feeling yet remained. Perhaps it always would. She might always have to live with his owning a piece of her heart.

She faced her brother. "If Jake will still have me, then I will marry him today as planned." That didn't answer his question, but it was the best she could do.

"What do you mean, 'if' Jake will marry you?" A scowl drew his brows together. "Don't tell me you're even thinking about telling him what happened tonight?"

"I have to. I can't begin this marriage with lies and deceit between us."

"Bullshit. There's nothing to tell him because nothing happened. Only you and I know what went on."

"And Donovan."

"That piece of shit won't say a word. You can count on that."

"Stop talking like that." She had never seen him quite so angry before.

"He won't ruin your future, Savannah. You will marry Jake today as scheduled. You can't let one innocent mistake jeopardize your happiness—or Reese's. If nothing else, think of your daughter."

Savannah had thought of no one else. What she had done tonight was something she would have warned Reese to never do. But she doubted Reese ever would: her daughter was smarter than her, had a well of common sense that Savannah had never possessed at that age. And apparently still didn't possess.

Deep down she felt that if she truly loved Jake as much as she wanted to, she wouldn't have done anything with Donovan. Perhaps she had sabotaged herself. She'd had doubts about marrying Jake from the start, but she'd pushed them down, believing it was past time that she settled down—and time to put the past behind her.

Reese deserved a home that consisted of a mother and father. Savannah knew she couldn't have picked a better man to give her daughter that than Jake.

"Go inside and get some sleep," Frank said in a gruff but calmer tone. "You've got a long day ahead of you."

Savannah didn't need anyone to tell her that, and she had much to sort out in only a few hours. "What are you going to do?"

A muscle worked in his jaw. "I'm not going to go looking for Jerricho, if that's what you're worried about."

That's exactly what she *was* worried about. "Are you angry with me?"

The tenseness seemed to leave his face. "How could I ever be angry with you?"

Tears suddenly welled up in her eyes and she wrapped her arms around her brother's neck. "I really screwed up, didn't I?"

"Yeah," he murmured in a rough, loving tone, hugging her back. "You really did." He took her gently by the arms and stepped back. "But don't think it can't be fixed. In a few days, this will all be an unfortunate memory and life will return to the way it's always been."

She tried to summon up a smile as she kissed Frank on the cheek, wearily climbed the steps, and entered the cool, apple-scented kitchen.

She leaned heavily against the closed door and wished time would stop until she could figure out how she could fix the mess she had made.

Donovan stared out the window of his old bedroom. The first rays of the sun were just peeking over the treetops and reflecting off Crawfish Lake.

He had always loved this place. Whenever his parents had been arguing, which had been frequently growing up, he would come here and hang out with his grandparents. When no one else understood him, they had.

They had also loved Savannah, seen in her what he had, and they had embraced her. He could only be thankful that they hadn't been around to see how badly he had screwed up his life.

He sighed and leaned his head against the glass, his mind replaying every moment of the hours he and Savannah had spent together.

God, how he had missed her. This was what he had refused to acknowledge all these years, because to do so had only brought legions of hurt.

No matter where he had gone or whom he had been with, his heart and soul belonged in Mississippi, with the only woman he had ever truly loved.

She had believed him to be asleep when she had risen from the bed in the middle of the night and taken off in his car. He hadn't stopped her because she needed to do what was right for her.

All night he had told himself that he would leave her alone. He'd go away again and let the past die once and for all. If she wanted to marry the doctor, then he had to stay out of it, no matter if he thought she was making an enormous mistake. No matter if he still loved her.

No matter if he wanted her for his wife.

Christ. He swung around and deliberately banged his head once against the wood frame, cursing his stupidity. He would call Nick to come and get him, then he'd pack up and head out. That was the plan. If he stayed, he would most likely do something stupid. Something Savannah might hate him for. Something that would feel damn good to him, though.

The sound of the front door slamming brought Donovan's head up and sparked his blood like a hot wire. Had Savannah returned? It had to be her; no one else knew where he was.

Donovan reached down to grab his shirt off the floor. When he straightened, he found Frank Harper on the threshold, dressed in black from the tip of his shit-kicker boots to the Stetson riding his head. Not a good start to the day.

The last time they had squared off, Donovan had broken Frank's nose, which still sported a slight cant, and Frank had managed to blacken Donovan's eye to the point where he couldn't open it for a week.

Donovan sat down on the edge of the windowsill and crossed his ankles. "I guess I don't need to ask why you're here."

Frank's hands curled into fists at his sides. "I warned you ten years ago to stay away from my sister, you son of a bitch."

"Are you conveying Savannah's request or your own?"

"Savannah's getting married today and I won't let anyone—especially you—ruin it for her. I told you the last time we crossed paths back in Detroit what I'd do if you ever came near my sister again." Frank put his hand behind his back and Donovan caught the glimmer of steel as Savannah's brother leveled a gun at him. "Perhaps you'll listen now."

"So you're going to kill me? You think that's a good idea?" Donavon asked calmly.

"I should have done it a long time ago. I should never have given you the chance to walk back into my sister's life."

"So when I'm dead and you're behind bars, who will be Savannah's fortress then? Who'll make sure nothing disrupts the hermetically sealed bubble you've put her in? And what'll happen to my daughter, Frank? Yeah, I see you're surprised. I know all about Reese, and if I was holding that gun, you might be the one contemplating the afterlife right now. I know it was you who told Savannah she was doing the right thing by keeping Reese from me."

The shock quickly wore off and a renewed determination lit Frank's eyes. "She told you that, did she?"

"She didn't have to. I know her better than you think.

She would never have kept this secret had you not been breathing down her neck." Donovan clamped his fingers around the windowsill. "She loves you, you know, though I haven't a fucking clue why."

"I am the only one who took care of Savannah, you asshole. You claimed to love her, but your dismissal nearly destroyed her. I was there to pick up the pieces while you were out screwing every whore you could lay your hands on."

"I'm sure that's what you want to believe, and I don't doubt that you fostered that notion in Savannah's head."

"Don't lay your guilt on my doorstep. You got what you deserved. You lost the best damn thing that would ever come your way, and I'm fucking glad. She was too good for you, but you couldn't see that. It was always all about you, the football hero. The Titan."

"You sound jealous."

"I don't want anything you have. Then I'd just be another low-life jock spreading my sperm across the states."

"As opposed to what you are now? Farmer in the dell and all that happy horse crap—sure you're fulfilled? Maybe if you had something going on in your own life, you wouldn't be so damn interested in your sister's."

"Maybe if you had a sister, you'd have a fucking clue. But you've got no one anymore, do you? You left your roots behind you to become someone important, but you're not so important now, are you?"

"No, I guess I'm not. So what's your beef, Frank? Are you blaming me because your bum knee kept you from going pro?"

"You just can't believe there's a life outside of football, can you? That was always your problem. You belonged to this exclusive jock club and no one was good enough to gain entrance, even Savannah."

Donovan gritted his teeth. "You know that's bullshit. My whole life was Savannah."

"Really. So you ignored her and then wondered why she would look to another man. She was pregnant and you were too self-absorbed to be there for her when she needed you."

"I tried to contact her, and you damn well know it. My letters came back. I suspect that was your doing."

"So if you thought all this, why didn't you tell Savannah?"

"Because I know she loves you, as misguided as you are."

Frank's grip tightened on the gun. "Misguided or not, you are history. Savannah's marrying Jake, a man who'll love her and Reese and treat my sister the way she deserves to be treated. Not fuck her and leave her, like you."

Donovan started toward Frank, wanting to wrap his hands around the bastard's throat and throttle him until he gurgled, but Frank cocked the trigger.

"Stay right there, unless you're hoping to be buried beneath the floorboards." He gestured with the pistol. "Now turn around and hold your hands out behind you."

Every muscle in Donovan's body ached to do injury to Savannah's brother. He was lying. He had been behind the scenes manipulating Savannah, but she loved him too much to see it.

Stiffly, Donovan pivoted around, his gaze centered on a picture on the wall as Frank came up behind him.

"This time I intend to make sure nothing interferes in my sister's life."

Donovan heard the swift rise of the pistol and tried to jerk around, but the gun butt slammed brutally against the back of his skull, his knees buckling as a consuming blackness took him down.

CHAPTER SEVEN

*S*avannah sat silently through the ordeal of getting her hair arranged. Marlene, her childhood friend and hairdresser, didn't notice as she talked a mile a minute, more excited than the bride-to-be about the upcoming nuptials. The bride-to-be had far more pressing concerns. She had not slept a wink; she had been too wracked with guilt and confusion.

As soon as was feasible, she had called Jake. But she had gotten his answering machine, and his cell phone was out of range.

She had forgotten that he and his best man, who was his brother, Jeff, had gone out fishing, wanting to have a few hours bonding.

Savannah summoned a smile and appropriate responses to Marlene's questions as she showed her friend to the door afterward, but had someone asked what she'd said or what had been said to her, Savannah would have drawn a complete blank.

Alone, she stood at her bedroom window hoping that

Jake would get her message. Until she spoke to him, she had to continue on as though nothing had changed, as though she had not just ruined what could have been a new beginning before she had even gotten the chance to start.

Savannah glanced to the west, toward the dense woods. Somewhere among the tall pines sat Magnolia Hills. And Donovan. Was he thinking about her? Was he happy that he'd proved she wasn't over him, as she had so steadfastly claimed?

Perhaps he had planned this seduction all along. Maybe it wasn't coincidence that he had appeared the day before she was to be married.

Savannah turned away from the window and closed her eyes. In the distance, she could hear the church bells chime, a hundred-year-old tradition that proclaimed a wedding would soon be taking place. A reminder that should have brought her joy. Dear God, what was she going to do?

"There's my angel," a male voice said.

Savannah turned to find Jake smiling in the doorway, but his smile faded as he caught the expression on her face. He crossed the room and gently laid his hands on her arms. It was all Savannah could do not to cry.

"What's the matter, honey? Don't tell me you've changed your mind?"

Though he said the words half-jokingly, Savannah felt her heart twist, explanations and apologies choking in her throat.

"I got your message," he said, his voice concerned as he

tugged her toward the bed and sat her down. "What is it? Has something happened? It is Reese? Is she all right?"

Savannah couldn't hold his gaze. "She's fine. This has nothing to do with Reese." But didn't it? Her actions had not only affected her life, but her daughter's as well. Perhaps, had she been thinking more of Reese than herself, none of this would have happened. "We have to talk."

He sat down beside her and cupped her jaw, turning her face to his. "You know you can say anything to me, don't you?"

Tears welled up behind Savannah's eyes and threatened to spill over. "Yes," she whispered. "You've always been a good friend to me. Better than I deserve at times."

"I hope to be more than just your friend. I want to be your partner, your confidant. A shoulder for you to cry on. Whatever you need."

He was so sweet, considerate, and kind, it was more than she could bear.

"You may not want me anymore, after what I have to say."

He paused. "I think I already know."

Savannah stared. "You do?"

"Does this have something to do with Donovan Jerricho?"

"How—"

"It's simple deduction. He's come home. I knew that."

"But you didn't say anything."

"What was I going to say? 'Don't talk to him. I don't want him here; I'm nervous about losing you. He's going to want you back. You may want him back. He was your first love.' Those kind of things?"

"Yes."

"What good would it have done me? I can't make you love me, Savannah. I understood what I was getting into, and you can't help who you love. I just wish it had been me. I wanted to take care of you and Reese, love you both the way I've been hoping to for a long time."

Her heart ached for him. "Jake . . ."

"I never told you, but I've had a crush on you since high school."

"You did?"

He gave her a boyish half grin. "I did. But you never noticed. Your eyes were for Donovan only."

He was right. Back then, she had seen little else. "I didn't set out to hurt you."

He brushed the hair back from her face. "I know, honey. I know." He took a breath and said, "So where do we go from here?"

Savannah rose from the bed and glanced out the window. She saw Frank pulling in, an agitated look about him as he exited his car, glancing back at it several times before his attention was diverted by her aunt Jessie.

Her aunt darted across the yard and began gesturing toward the house. Savannah didn't have to read lips to figure out what her aunt was saying.

As though on cue, Frank's gaze shot to her bedroom window. He had just learned that Jake was there, despite his order that she was to act as though nothing had happened. But she couldn't deceive someone she cared for.

She dearly loved her brother and would always appreciate

how he had held her together after Donovan. But she was older now—and hopefully wiser. She had her own ways of doing things; she just couldn't get him to see that.

Her brother marched toward the house, and Savannah figured she had about two minutes to say what she had to say.

Taking a deep breath, she faced Jake. "If you want to call off the wedding, I'll understand."

Jake rose from the bed and walked toward her. When he stood before her, softly dappled in a ray of midmorning sun, he said, "No, I don't want to call off the wedding. I love you, Savannah. I know whatever happened between you and Jerricho was . . ." He shrugged, struggling to find the right words. "Let's call it a onetime mistake that will never be repeated. I don't want to throw everything away because of one error."

The tears Savannah had tried to hold back spilled over her lashes. "You don't have it in you to hate anyone, do you?"

"Hate is a waste of time." He cupped the back of her neck and drew her toward him. "But I don't hate you, if that's what you're worried about. I could never hate you. I don't blame you for whatever may have transpired between you and Jerricho. I know you love me." He bent his knees and came down to her level, looking her in the eyes to say, "You do, Savannah, don't you?"

It all came down to this, Savannah thought, a terrible, encompassing numbness settling over her skin, the truth welling up inside her, telling her all the things she had already known but refused to acknowledge.

She laid her palm against Jake's cheek. "I care so deeply about you. You've been a wonderful friend to me and Reese."

"But you don't love me."

"Don't, Savannah," came Frank's warning voice from the doorway, his eyes glinting with anger.

"I have to do what's right, Frank."

"Then think about Reese."

"I am thinking about her. Are you?"

"Are you implying that I don't care about my own niece? I've been a surrogate father to her."

"She has a real father. It's not fair to him. I only wish I'd seen that sooner."

"Reese's father is alive?"

Savannah glanced up at Jake. He had taken so many blows and had remained faithful to his vow to her. She knew she couldn't pretend to be what he needed. He deserved so much more.

"Yes . . . Reese's father is alive."

"Jerricho."

Savannah closed her eyes and inclined her head.

"Well," Jake said on a weary sigh, "I guess that says everything."

"I'm sorry," she whispered, her throat tight with emotion. No matter how she felt about Donovan, she had given a piece of her heart to Jake. His friendship had meant so much to her. She didn't want to lose it, but knew nothing would ever be the same.

"Come on, Jake," Frank said in a cajoling tone with a

forced edge. "She's just been under a strain. We all have. You two can't just walk away from each other. Not because of Jerricho. He's history anyway."

His remark sent a jolt through Savannah. "What have you done, Frank? Please tell me you kept your word and left him alone."

Frank's eyes narrowed on her. "He's the cause of all your problems and yet you're worried about him? Jesus, Savannah, wake up."

"I am awake, Frank. Perhaps more than I've been in the last eight years. Whether Donovan stays or goes, I know who I am now, and I know what I want. I can't spend the rest of my life pretending that things never changed. Reese deserves to know her father, if he wants to know her."

"I do." The reply seemed to come out of nowhere.

Frank wrenched around and found Donovan standing behind him in the hallway. A single punch to the jaw laid her brother out flat.

Savannah gasped and knelt down at her brother's side.

"He'll be fine," Donovan said through a split lip that had undoubtedly resulted from his hitting the hardwood floor in his bedroom.

He had awoken in the trunk of Frank's car, a rag shoved in his mouth and his wrists and ankles bound like a convicted felon's.

His injured arm hurt like a son of a bitch from throwing his weight up against the trunk lid, and he cradled it protectively in front of him.

He'd finally been released by Savannah's aunt, who looked shocked at finding him a prisoner in Frank's trunk. Donovan would probably never know why Savannah's brother hadn't killed him, as he had threatened, why he had driven home, instead. But Donovan took it as a sign he had no intention of ignoring.

Savannah looked up at him with an accusatory glare, but then her expression suddenly changed.

"You're bleeding. And your arm's hurt."

"You can thank your brother for that. You might request that he be a little less zealous in his protection of you. Your future husband may not like it."

Jake obviously took that as a prompt. "The infamous Donovan Jerricho," he said from across the room, looking more curious than intimidated.

"The infamous pediatrician, Dr. Jake . . . ?"

"Marshall," he answered. "And I doubt anyone thinks I'm infamous. My patients only know me as the man who gives them candy after a shot. Nothing nearly as glorious as being a pro footballer."

"Ex-footballer."

"Ah, yes. It looks like your arm's still troubling you. If you'd like to stop by my office sometime, I have a hydro-bath that's quite therapeutic."

"You're joking, right?"

"Not at all."

Donovan leaned his shoulder against the doorjamb and shook his head. "Has anyone told you that you're too damn nice?"

A half grin tipped up the corners of Jake's mouth. "It's a fatal flaw, I suppose."

"Are you two finished?" Savannah asked in an exasperated tone as she held her brother's head in her lap.

"Here, let me take him." Jake came over and slid his arm beneath her brother's shoulders, then attempted to heft him off the ground.

Donovan reached down and put his arm under Frank's other side. Together, the two men lifted her brother to his feet, still groggy from the blow.

"Let's get him to a bed."

Savannah watched as all the men in her life exited the room, leaving her there alone on what was to have been her wedding day. Well, why should anything be any different? She seemed destined to be alone.

"Can I come in?"

Startled by Donovan's voice, Savannah jumped to her feet. "You shouldn't be here. Jake will be back in a minute."

"I don't think so. He's taking Frank to his office."

Savannah heard the roar of an engine and raced to the window in time to see Jake's car leaving the driveway, her brother slumped on the seat next to him.

Donovan gently turned her to face him. "I still love you, Savannah. I tried to stay away, but I couldn't."

"You managed it quite well for a long time."

"I was an ass. A stupid, immature kid who had been handed the world and didn't know what to do with it."

"So you think you know better now, do you?"

He lightly skimmed a finger along her cheek. "I think so,

but I could still use some help. If you tell me that you don't love me, I'll leave and never darken your doorstep again."

Savannah willed herself to say the words. She could list at least twenty reasons why it was a bad idea to allow him back into her life. She should run as far and fast as she could—but her feet were glued to the floor.

"I don't love you, Donovan. I'm sorry. It's over for me."

He said nothing, but she recognized the devastation in his eyes. She had seen that same look in her own eyes for months after he had left. Hurt beyond words. A vast emptiness that nothing could fill.

She had never thought he would feel it, and she had certainly never believed she would be around to witness it. Instead of any satisfaction, a terrible hollowness sank deep inside her.

"Take care of yourself," he said, his gaze holding hers for a long moment before he turned and left the room.

Savannah stood rooted to the floor, her heart beating wildly, her lie ringing in her ears. She had done the right thing, she told herself over and over as his footsteps echoed down the hallway, then the steps, as the front door opened and closed, as his boots crunched over the gravel drive, heading away from her house—and out of her life forever.

Suddenly she felt unbearable grief at the thought of never seeing him again and ran from her room, her breath rasping in her lungs as she threw open the front door and flew down the driveway.

"Wait!" she called out.

Donovan stopped at the end of the driveway, but did not

turn around. Savannah slowed as she neared him, coming to a halt a few feet away.

"Please look at me."

"I can't." The hurt was so real in his voice that it struck her like a dagger.

With tentative steps, she came around to stand in front of him, shocked to find tears in his eyes. In all the years she had known him, he had never cried.

She reached up and wiped her thumb across his cheek. He captured her hand and held it there, staring down at her, and within that beautiful blue gaze, she saw the boy she had once loved so desperately. She had believed he had been lost forever.

He wouldn't help her. Wouldn't give her a single word to make it easier for her to say what she had chased him down to say.

But suddenly, her fear melted away. The truth was, she still loved him. Had always loved him. Would never stop loving him.

She wanted to face the rest of her life with him at her side. She had to know if it could ever be the way she had dreamed it could.

Rising up on tiptoe, she looped her arms around his neck, her kiss conveying all the love that had never left her.

And in that kiss, she knew she had made the right decision. The world had become new again, and with it, she had found a promise of forever.

HUNTER'S RIGHT

Jaid Black

Verily, a time of great suffering shall fall upon the whole of the world, for its women will dwindle in numbers. Disease shall soon spread, female babes will not be born, and bloodlines will die out. But, yea, the strong Vikings shall live on, for almighty Odin has seen fit to warn us. We are His chosen people.

Take to the earth, the haven bequeathed to us; the belly of the gods. Dwell below her dirt and leaves, now and forever, untouched by the Outsiders and their ways. Yea, let each warrior cling unto a wife, that his seed may bear fruit and our race prevail. Should a time come when there are fewer females than warriors in our stronghold, then hunt on the Outside and take them.

By any means necessary, take them.

—Viking legend

CHAPTER ONE

Arctic seacoast
Present day

*I*t was turning out to be one hell of a long day. The flight schedule had begun at the crack of dawn. She'd flown from Dulles Airport in Washington, D.C., to Seattle in Washington State, then onward to Fairbanks, Alaska. In Fairbanks, a military chopper had picked her up. The team was currently en route to their destination: nowhere. Almost literally. The highly classified army complex that operated just north of the Arctic circle was top secret and could only be reached in one of two ways: by helicopter, as they were currently approaching it, or by dogsled.

Corporal Ronda Tipton of the U.S. Army blinked her eyelids rapidly to keep from falling asleep. How she could doze off in a loud military chopper was beyond comprehension, but it had been an exhausting day. By the time the aircraft landed, her journey would be seventeen hours from start to finish.

Staring out the small window on her left to the beautiful winterscape below, Ronda's mind alternated between fatigue and excitement. This was the first invigorating assignment she'd had in ages. Her last several years in the army had been on the dull, paper-pushing side of things. All computers and paperwork—no action.

That state of affairs, however, had been inevitable after she'd taken a bullet to the kneecap from a guerrilla's gun in Haiti. Helping two fellow soldiers get to safety had made her something of a hero, but it had also retired her from active duty and landed her with a desk job. Her knee had long since healed, but returning to the field was still out. She'd never pass the army's stringent physical requirements for active combat or for any assignment that required more than minimal risk.

Now, at age thirty-three, Ronda was more than ready to shake up her mundane nine-to-five existence, if even just for a little while. When her boss had offered her the opportunity to oversee a classified military project in the Arctic circle, she'd jumped at the chance. She had joined the army to see the world and to make a difference, not to sit behind a desk accepting and rejecting expenditures for the military's budget.

"What the . . . ?" Ronda's brown eyes widened as she was suddenly jarred back and forth in her small seat. "What's going on?" she shouted over the loud buzz of the helicopter's engine—and over the sound of rotary blades grinding against each other.

Her heart stilled. Something was very wrong. Ronda had

been a passenger on more chopper rides than she could count, and she'd never experienced anything like this. The jumping, jarring, and plummeting went way beyond turbulence.

Her heart began to race. With both hands, she clutched the safety harness that came over her head and across her chest until her knuckles turned white. "What is going on!" she yelled again, much louder and more demanding this time. *"Lieutenant?"*

Suddenly there was the horrific grinding sound of shredding metal, and all hell broke loose.

"Hold on, we're going down!"

"Oh, Jesus—send aid! Command—this is Phantom III—send aid!"

"Oh my God!" Ronda clutched the harness impossibly tighter. Blood pounded in her ears. Perspiration drenched her forehead and dripped down the side of her face. Her teeth rattled together from the helicopter's frenetic bumping.

The chopper was out of control. The small four-seater was being jarred and bumped in so many directions, she could no longer tell up from down or left from right. All she knew was that the snowcapped mountains of ice that had seemed so distant were now suddenly, horrifically, spiraling into bone-chilling view.

OhmyGodohmyGodohmyGod . . .

The chopper made impact, crashing into the side of a mountain coated with unforgiving ice.

We're going to die! Oh my God—nooooo!

It was Ronda's last coherent thought. Then, mercifully, blackness engulfed her until she knew no more.

She had no idea how long she'd been unconscious. When Ronda pulled herself up from under the wreckage that had once been a part of Phantom III, groaning like the wounded animal she felt to be, she surmised that more than a day had passed. Call it intuition, call it an educated guess, or call it the painful knot that had formed on the side of her head, but she was certain she'd been knocked out cold for a day or two.

Delicately probing her head for further injuries, she quickly ascertained that she had sustained only the single wound at her left temple. Ronda winced as her fingers grazed over the tender lump. She knew enough about basic survival to realize that, while painful, the knot was not deadly. Dried blood was in the golden curls at her hairline, but she felt no shards of metal in the wound.

Though the injury to her head probably wouldn't kill her, the bitter cold snow surrounding her for as far as the eye could see might. She needed help, food, and medical supplies.

Where am I?

Ronda's gaze anxiously darted around, searching for other survivors. Her forehead wrinkled as she noted that the remaining wreckage was much more sparse than it should have been. A piece of metal here, a part of a blade there . . .

She stilled. And then, knowing and simultaneously dreading the answer, she weakly dragged her feet toward the edge of the snowy shelf she'd awoken on.

She moved slowly, cautiously, testing each inch of snow, not sure what was solid mountain and what was white fluff that would disintegrate under her feet—and send her plummeting below. Finally glancing over the ice-coated cliff, she drew in a deep breath as she visually confirmed what she'd hoped her mind had been wrong about. Sorrow for men she barely knew hit her like a punch to the belly.

The others were all gone. She was the only survivor.

Ronda could barely see what was left of Phantom III, but her army-trained eyes honed in on the fact that nobody— *nobody*—could have survived that crash. The chopper had fallen too fast and too many thousands of feet below for any of the crew to have escaped certain death. Bloodstained snow and shredded metal were scattered everywhere.

Ronda shivered, her teeth chattering, as reality set in. The coldness of the snowy mountainside she was stranded on seeped though the protection of her army-issued snowsuit and into her bones.

She was alone—all alone. Any flares she might have launched to signal her position had probably gone down with the larger portion of Phantom III and its ill-fated crew.

How did I survive?

Her seat must have ripped away from the main cabin of the aircraft. How, she'd never know.

Now what was of utmost importance was the need to survive. She'd made it this far. She owed it to herself, as well as to the family members of the crew, to get to safety and to tell the army where the men's remains were located.

Backing away from the dizzying view below, Ronda

quickly went to rummage through the small bits of Phantom III left on the plateau of ice. Moving so briskly made the pain at the side of her head sting fiercely; she hissed, but otherwise ignored the throbbing at her temple as she poked around the helicopter's remains.

Nothing. Not a flare, not a radio, not even a solitary bandage or a crumb of bread. Nothing.

She sighed, her eyes briefly closing before flicking back open. "What do I do now?" Ronda whispered. "Think, girl. Think."

There was but one course of action: find a way off this mountain, and find it now.

Easier said than done.

Ronda sat on a sizable boulder nearby, leaned back against the snowy mountain, and tried to figure out just how in the world she would get out of this nightmare. She wasn't Superwoman—she couldn't fly off the damn thing like some comic-book hero. And without the proper equipment, she couldn't climb down off of it, either. Which left her . . .

Sitting right where she was.

A part of Ronda morbidly wondered if she'd have been better off going down with Phantom III. At least the other crew members had died on impact. She was facing starvation, hypothermia, and a painfully slow death.

Jaw tight, Ronda forced herself back up to her feet. "I'm not dying like this!" she yelled, her voice echoing throughout the mountains. She took a deep, icy breath and expelled it, realizing how stupid it was to holler out her frustration and fear when nobody would hear it. She needed to conserve her energy for whatever lay ahead.

"I'm not dying like this," she repeated more quietly. In active duty—okay. While in enemy territory—okay. But not standing on a cold, lonely mountaintop. Turning to face the boulder, she sank one booted foot in a crevice near its base, leaned a palm against the solid mountain wall to her left, and tried to think. There *had* to be a way off this mountain.

Both of Ronda's parents had died as military heroes: her mother in Russia during the Cold War, her father several years ago in Afghanistan. As a child, the loss of her mom had been a kid's worst nightmare realized. As an adult, the death of her dad had been more tragic still, for she'd lived with him and loved him for so much longer. Ronda's only consolation at their funerals was knowing they had died as honored American heroes. Nothing less than what either of them would have wanted.

She didn't want to be a hero if it meant dying. Odd as it might sound coming from a career military woman, she wasn't a pro-war person. She believed that the function of the armed forces should be defensive only—to protect and defend the country, that Americans might know peace and safety. She didn't agree with quite a few stances the military had taken over the years, but she wisely kept her mouth shut and her job intact.

The payoff was this assignment: a top-secret experiment that might just, after thousands of years of war, bring peace to the entire planet. Her role here, as a paper-pushing geek with an eye for budgets and enough finesse to talk the Pentagon into spending whatever funds were necessary, wasn't particularly exciting. But the project itself was the most exciting work she'd had in years. And now, because of it, she was facing a slow, painful death.

"What do I do?" Ronda removed her hand from the mountain wall, absently watching snow fall from where her glove had once rested. "Maybe I—"

Her dark brown eyes narrowed, a frown marring her features. *What the . . .*

Her hand flew back to the mountain wall, and she quickly brushed more snow away. Ronda sucked in her breath when she realized that behind the snow sat a stone door.

A door?

Of course! Phantom III must have crashed directly atop the secret military compound! But then, why hadn't army soldiers come to her rescue? Maybe the compound sat toward the mountain's root and nobody had heard the crash?

It didn't matter. Ronda's heart was pounding with too much adrenaline to care. Where there was a door, there was bound to be a civilization—and food and warmth and medical supplies. Hope surged inside her.

She would live! Against all odds, she would survive.

The door resisted her efforts to open it. She marched back to the remains of the chopper and found a piece of metal that would work as a crowbar. Where there was a will, there was also a way.

Ronda excitedly set to work, methodically prying the

stone door open from behind the boulder. Her muscles burned and her teeth gritted from the labor, but she didn't relent. A smile of victory and relief curved her lips when the stone door finally yielded. Not much, but she was pretty sure she'd jacked it open far enough to get in.

Throwing the makeshift crowbar to the ground, Ronda squeezed through the tight portal.

Chapter Two

*I*t was dark inside the mountain. It took Ronda's eyes several moments to adjust to the atmosphere. Even then, there was only so much adjusting retinas could do in pitch-blackness.

"Hello?" she called out. Her voice echoed off the walls. "Is anybody in here?"

Silence.

"Hello? I'm Corporal Ronda Tipton of the United States army. Can anybody hear me?"

Again, silence.

Obviously she was too high up for anyone to hear her. She'd have to inch her way down the mountain. One thing was for certain—it was definitely warmer inside the mountain than outside it. She knew in her gut that signaled civilization. It had to.

Whoever had received their distress signal probably assumed that all the passengers of Phantom III had died on impact. How surprised they'd be to see her walking down the passageway that had neatly been carved inside the mountain. Now, if only she could actually find her way down it . . .

Ronda put her hands up in front of her and slowly walked forward. When she felt a wall, she took off her right glove, stuffed it into a pocket, and used that hand to feel her way down. She kept her left hand in front of her so as not to bump into any barriers.

For the next hour, Ronda wound farther and farther down the mountain. She stayed steady, keeping at a snail's pace, so as not to cause further injury to herself. After what felt like half of forever, she finally saw light up ahead. It was dim, but it was definitely light. *Yes!*

"Keep it steady, Ronda," she murmured to herself. "No tripping."

The urge to bolt toward the light was strong. She resisted it, even though this slow shuffling was driving her mad. But she'd carefully inched her way down the spiral of the mountain interior for over an hour. She could resist the temptation to run for another few minutes.

Finally—finally!—she got close enough to the dim light to walk a bit faster, and without needing to use her hands as guides. She still couldn't move too hastily, though, for the footing had become trickier. Another half hour, and Ronda was at last inside the mountain chamber that was emitting the light.

Her eyes widened. *What in the world . . . ?*

In the mountain's belly was a hollowed-out cavity that contained twenty huge pits of some boiling substance. Wax? Oil? She didn't know. It wasn't the right color to be lava, so *people* had put the substance inside the man-made pits, which looked too crude to be army-made. They were well crafted, but lacked the technical appearance of military manufacturing.

"Kom och titta på det här!"

The booming male voice startled Ronda. That he wasn't speaking English sent warning bumps down her spine. Military-bred instincts taking over, she jumped behind the closest boulder to hide and found a crack to watch through.

Oh my God.

A six-and-a-half-foot-tall man in his fifties made his way into the cavern with a cloaked woman who appeared to be in her eighties or nineties. The old woman dressed and looked like your average crone out of a movie—nothing too shocking there. But the man? He was dressed like . . .

A Viking. Yes, that's what he resembled—some ancient Nordic warrior! Long, white-blond hair plaited at the temples, two bangles with dragon heads clasped unforgivingly around both bulging biceps, no shirt, brown leather brais for pants, huge musculature.

He was terrifying looking.

Ronda watched the conversation between the giant man and the old woman with intense curiosity. Who were these people? What were they doing here? The only non-English-speaking peoples she knew of in this remote area were the Inuit Eskimos, and most of them spoke English too.

The old woman nodded. "Det ser bra ut för min del."

"Så det är klart då?"

"Ja."

Ja. The old woman had phonetically said *yah.* That *was* a Nordic word! Swedish? Norwegian?

This was getting stranger by the second.

"Kom. Vi går tillbaka." The man led the old, cloaked woman from the chamber. "Jag ska hämta några krigare så vi kan ta tillbaka det."

"Perfekt."

As they disappeared, Ronda had but a split second to decide to follow them or not. Though something quite bizarre was going on here, these people might also be her only way out of the mountain.

She decided to follow, but to keep a safe distance between her and them. She didn't want to alert them to her presence until she knew more about who they were, what they were doing, and why they were here. Maybe they were just two harmless people who lived in the rough terrain of the Arctic and used this mountain for boiling waxes and oils—or something. Though that didn't explain the male's weird manner of dress.

Wherever Ronda was following them to, it was becoming warmer by the second. And louder; she could hear the clang of metal striking metal. As she continued to trail the duo, ducking behind this rock and that, the sound of voices caught her ear, all speaking that foreign tongue.

Ronda rounded a bend, then ducked behind a large boulder next to a stone wall as she watched the old woman and her escort make their way to a crude iron-wrought elevator. As the caged elevator went down, large bars of metal acting as counterweights rose up.

Clearly this was no army complex. Taking a deep breath and quietly exhaling, Ronda worked up her nerve to peer over the stone wall and see what lay below it. When she did, her jaw dropped open in disbelief.

"This can't be real," she whispered. "A primitive city?"

In science fiction movies, whenever earthlings found a planet with other humanoid life-forms, the discovered civilization was primitive in some ways and advanced in other ways—exactly like the city below. The foundation of the settlement was stone, mud, and huts, yet the people were advanced enough to fashion caged elevators and what looked like weapons.

Ronda wondered if she was the first person from the outside world to ever lay eyes on this civilization. After all, the colony was in the middle of nowhere, existing below some of the most rugged and frigid terrain on earth.

Like an awe-filled kid who'd just found Santa's hiding place at the north pole, Ronda studied everything she could see. This main atrium had several levels, and they went down so many thousands of feet that she could only make out what lay on the upper five.

The fifth and fourth levels looked like primitive shopping malls with huts and booths that resembled stalls more than actual stores. It brought to mind a Hawaiian flea market or Covent Garden in London—except that the people dressed like they'd just walked out of a history book, and the shoppers appeared to barter for what they wanted rather than buy it outright. Apparently money wasn't used here.

Does the army know about this place? Does anyone?

The third level up was also a place to shop—but, sweet Lord, what was being sold was too incredible to believe! If she hadn't seen it with her own eyes—

"Oh my God," Ronda breathed out. "This isn't happening." The huge, Viking-dressed males on the third level up were bartering for . . .

Women. *Naked* women! And, what was worse, by the manner in which the women of various colors were being cajoled toward the stage in shackled feet, Ronda knew they were unwilling auction chattel.

Ronda's hand flew up to cover her mouth. This just couldn't be real.

She wasn't able to make out what was being said by anybody on the third level. It was too far away to hear anything, and the sounds competed against the loud clanging of metal striking metal on the second level.

A nude, redheaded woman with fair skin was dragged, kicking and screaming, to the center of the platform by two huge men. Her large breasts bobbed up and down as she tried to break free from their hold, to no avail. It was like watching a squirming fish try to elude two hungry bears. The guards held her still while twenty potential buyers boldly inspected her. They forced her mouth open to scrutinize her teeth, ran their hands over her large breasts with extended pink nipples, and—

Ronda couldn't bear to watch anymore.

Scared and shaking, she knew if she was captured by these people, she might find herself up on one of those very platforms.

"Keep it together, girlfriend," she murmured. "You've made it this far."

She'd survived at least ten ambushes in her life, the death of two parents, and a helicopter crash. She could survive this too. She just had to think of what to do.

The quiet before the storm.

The thought entered her mind from seemingly nowhere, and it took her a second to figure out why. The clanging sound of metal striking metal had abruptly stopped. She blinked.

Her gaze flew down to the now quiet second floor from her hiding place. She stilled, even as her heart began to pound against her chest. "Holy shit," Ronda muttered.

They knew she was here. Approximately fifty Viking men had ceased their blacksmith work and were staring up at her, all of them clearly alerted to her presence somehow.

This is NOT happening!

Swallowing against the lump of fear in her throat that felt the size of an apple, Ronda's wide brown eyes clashed with acutely intense blue ones. Her heart began pounding impossibly harder, beads of perspiration dotting her forehead.

The giant who'd snared her gaze made her mouth go cotton dry. His body was as formidable as his eyes. It was hard to judge from this height just how huge he was, but he had to be as tall or taller than the first man she'd seen—at least six and a half feet. And powerfully, heavily muscled.

His hair was dark brown and fell to the middle of his back. A braid at either temple had been pulled to the back of his head and knotted there to keep his hair out of his eyes. He wore only black leather brais, black boots, and a huge gold bangle clasped around each obscenely bulging biceps. No shirt to cover that massive chest or those vein-roped arms, which made him look even more frightening.

He was watching her, assessing her, sizing her up as if calculating every possible move she might make toward escape. She had fought against the deadliest of enemies during her field years, but this was the first man she'd ever gone up against whose mere stare made every hair at the nape of her neck stand on end. His ice blue eyes were as penetrating and merciless looking as the rugged, bitter cold terrain outside. And those eyes were watching *her*.

When she'd decided her life needed some excitement, this was *not* what she'd had in mind!

"Let go of me! You goddamn bastard—*let go!*"

Because the sound of clanging metal had ceased while all eyes were on her, Ronda heard the redheaded woman's English-spoken cry from far below. Ronda's gaze flew to the naked, shackled female whose breasts were being rubbed and kneaded by two large hands. Her heartbeat racing, Ronda then returned her gaze to the giant who stood just one level below her.

The big man's cold blue gaze glanced pointedly downward, then slowly back up to look Ronda in the eyes. A half smile twisted his lips.

Oh, no—oh, God!

Ronda's entire body began to shake. He was telling her without words what he intended to happen to her.

Hell, *no!*

Breaking out of her frozen shock, Ronda whipped around and bolted back toward the cavern that contained the boiling liquid.

"Ta henne!"

She heard the battle cry, clearly an order to capture her. Then loud footfalls pounding, and the iron-caged elevator ascending toward the uppermost level.

What do I do now? Where do I go!

There was nothing outside to run to but a ten-thousand-foot drop off an icy cliff.

"Help me, God," Ronda panted, running so fast it made her dizzy. "Please."

As she reached the cavern filled with the pits of boiling fluid, her wild gaze darted about the rocky chamber for a hiding place. She espied a small, cramped space between two boulders and quickly squeezed her body in. Forcibly steadying her breathing, she remained as still as a statue. All she could do now was wait.

And hope they didn't find her.

CHAPTER THREE

*S*tay calm. Do not move. Do not breathe if you can help it. Stay calm . . .

Ronda repeated the mental mantra over and over, half-wondering if she was dreaming all this from a hospital bed. The sound of booming male voices jarred her back to reality.

The Viking men had entered the chamber.

Please don't let them find me. God—please!

They talked amongst themselves, but she had no idea what they were saying. As the chamber became brighter, she guessed the men had lit some torches and were preparing to climb the spiral of the mountain to the top. She waited with infinite patience until the voices became mere echoes in the distance, then slowly, quietly, unwedged herself from between the rocks.

Prepared for a surprise attack, she took her time, careful not to get taken unaware. But no one was in the chamber.

Her best chance of escape was to go down rather than up—the last thing the enemy would expect her to do.

The one thing she least wanted to do.

Carefully tiptoeing toward the cavern entrance that would lead to the elevator, Ronda kept her eyes and ears on full alert. Ready to proceed with operation Get Me the Fuck Outta Here, she took off running, rounded a corner—and slammed smack-dab into the middle of a massive, muscular chest. She fell to the ground, landing on her backside.

Ronda gasped and looked up, the pain in her wounded head so blinding it made her cry out.

It was *him*—the giant. And, oh, boy, was he even bigger and deadlier looking up close. His heavily muscled body was tensed for battle. His face was a mask of fury, cold blue eyes narrowed into merciless slits.

Survival instincts taking over, Ronda put her weight on her left knee in a lightning-fast movement and karate-kicked her enemy in the groin with her right leg.

He bellowed in pain and anger as he fell to his knees. Her heart pounding so fast it felt as though it might beat out of her chest, Ronda darted past him. He howled as she ran by, sending goose bumps zinging down her spine.

Run faster! Faster! Faster! Faster!

Adrenaline rushed through her, and she dashed toward the elevator. The pain in her head was horrific, but getting caught by these sadists would be far worse.

Almost there!

As Ronda reached out to open the cage doors, two rough, calloused hands grabbed her by the back of the shoulders.

No!

She elbowed him in the gut. He grunted and released her. She dropped to the floor to deliver another kick to the groin, but he took her by surprise and went down to the floor with her. They wrestled for a moment, Ronda fighting like a wildcat.

"Let go of me!" she raged, clawing and hitting at him.

The giant got on top of her and pinned her hands to the ground over her head. He used his massive weight to subdue her, situating himself intimately between her thighs. She could feel the bulge of his erection pressing against her despite the black leather brais and army-green snowsuit that lay between them.

"Who are you?" the giant hissed in heavily accented English, his voice deep and angry. Those icy blue eyes sparked with fire and his nostrils flared, making his features appear impossibly more menacing. "Tell me!" he ground out, releasing her hands to seize two fistfuls of her golden hair by the roots.

Pain seared Ronda's head wound and she cried out. Dizziness and nausea assailed her. The fear of death loomed hauntingly close.

"P-please," she gasped. "Please d-don't hurt me anymore."

Nikolas's jaw tensed as he stared down into the beautiful but cunning face of his quarry. He thought she might be feigning injury to surprise him with another attack, but then he saw the wound. He immediately released her hair and pinned her hands above her head once again.

"Who are you?" he repeated, slower this time in case she couldn't understand his English. "How did you find this colony?" His teeth all but gnashed together. *"Who sent you here?"*

"My n-name is R-Ronda Tipton," she gasped out. "I'm a corporal with the United States army."

Nikolas's stomach clenched. The Outsiders' warriors knew of this place? Damn Toki!

"Why were you sent here?" he demanded harshly. "Tell me!"

She blinked. "Sent here?" she whispered, her voice weak and pained.

"Little girl," he murmured, his temper barely restrained, " 'Tis smart to give me the answers I seek." His hands gripped hers tighter. He would get the old herbalist to mend her injury once she told him what he needed to know.

"Please," she said softly, her face scrunched up into a mask of pain, "I don't know what you are talking ab-bout. We were en route to a secret military base just north of the Arctic circle. The helicopter c-crashed into the mountain. I'm the only survivor."

Nikolas stilled. He recalled a trembling of the entire colony that none could explain. Yet that had been two moon-risings ago.

He examined her wound more closely. Indeed, the head injury was not fresh. 'Twas at least a couple of moon-risings old.

He studied her face. She was as striking up close as he'd thought her to be from afar, beguilingly so. Her eyes were dark and beautiful, her hair a rich gold. Her nose was perfect for her face, neither too large nor too small. Her cheekbones were high and delineated, her lips full and richly colored.

Was it possible this "Ronda" spoke the truth? Or did her beauty make him want to believe she was but an innocent who'd unknowingly stumbled upon the stronghold of New Sweden? It was in a man's nature to want to believe that a wench so fine of face was just as fine of character.

He would have Otrygg hunt for the remains of an Outsider's flying bird. Until then, he would reserve judgment.

"I'll carry you to a healer," Nikolas told her. One dark brown eyebrow slowly rose. "If you attempt to thwart me again, I will show you no mercy."

But the warning was of no consequence, for she had passed out cold.

CHAPTER FOUR

Two days later

*N*ikolas Ericsson removed his tunic and tossed it on a nearby hook after entering the grindstone. 'Twas smoldering hot within the highest-working echelon of New Sweden.

The grindstone was divided into two sectors. On one side, raw metals were hammered into tradable goods. On the other side, mined gemstones were cleaned for bartering. Nikolas owned the grindstone outright—not through inheritance, but due to hard work and determination on his part. 'Twas mayhap why he took the time to oversee his men and help them where needed. He carried no airs about him as many overlords did.

"Niko!"

Nikolas nodded at Otrygg, acknowledging him. Otrygg was one of his most trusted men and supporters. When the inevitable clash for ultimate power between Nikolas and Toki came, he knew he could count on Otrygg to stand beside him and fight.

Toki Ericsson was Nikolas's cousin. Toki, the clan's current jarl, was mayhap his sire's heir in bloodline, but not in spirit. It had been the dead jarl's dying wish to Nikolas that his nephew depose Toki as ruler and claim the kingship for himself.

Verily, he could empathize with his dearly departed uncle. Toki was crazed of the mind and given to bloodlust. His treatment of captured brides on the customary marriage auction block was more like chattel than revered soon-to-be wives. Additionally, he had nigh unto given up the clan's underground position twice now.

For over a thousand years the various clans of New Norway, New Daneland, and New Sweden had existed without interference from Outsiders because naught was known of the clans' existence. 'Twas how it was supposed to be. 'Twas how the gods and goddesses had decreed it to be.

In a couple more decades, those who lived above the ground would not escape the wrath of the gods for destroying their territory and perverting the laws of the natural world. Only those below the ground would survive, flourish, and prosper.

"Good day," Nikolas rumbled out to Otrygg.

"Milord." Otrygg respectfully inclined his white-blond head. "I believe two more of the oil pits are ready. I will take Old Myria up to inspect them."

Oils were precious and bartered for high, as they could be used to make everything from soaps to perfumes to foodstuffs. It would bring the resistance more weapons.

"You can't take her up to the pits today." Nikolas resumed walking toward the blacksmiths to see if he could be of assistance. "Take her daughter instead," he threw out over his shoulder. "Myria is still attending to my captive's injuries."

Otrygg bowed to Nikolas's back before leaving.

Soon Nikolas was busy laboring alongside his men, pounding metals into workable material. His muscles tensed and bulged with every strike of hammer against metal. Sweat glistened on his naked chest; his forehead was soaked with the dampness of exertion.

'Twas just as it had been two eves past when he had first spotted *her*—his captive. He thought about Ronda as he toiled, hoping her fever had broken since he'd last seen her.

She wouldn't know it until she woke up, but Ronda would never be leaving this colony. She couldn't. Too much was at stake for their people to lose should Outsiders come to know of the Underground settlements.

Nikolas had given up a lot in life that he might concentrate on fulfilling the promise he had made to his dying uncle. Verily, he should already have taken a wife and begun the furthering of his line. Instead, he had spent his life learning how to fight, how to be the deadliest warrior the colonies had ever known. The past three years had been spent gaining supporters, developing superior weaponry to that of Toki and his warriors, and plotting with his most trusted allies to overthrow the mad jarl.

Nikolas had now seen thirty-six years. At times he got to feeling lonely, but such was the price a man paid for the greater good. Leastways, 'twas the price a warrior paid when he cared for his people. He would not marry until New Sweden was safely under his control.

Nikolas hoped Ronda had no husband and children in the world above the ground. Having seen such a situation occur once before with a captive named Meg, he remembered how overly long it had taken her to accept that she had a new husband and that she could never leave—she'd spent months, mayhap even years, hoping her first husband would find her and take her back above ground.

Such was why bride hunters did all they could to ensure that the women they stole were not already mated. In this case, no bride hunters had been involved. The wench had unwittingly stumbled upon New Sweden's stronghold. And Ronda, married by Outsider laws or not, would be sent to the marriage auction block, just as all unwed women were.

No law in New Sweden could save her from the inevitable, since no law in the Underground recognized the ceremonies of Outsiders as legally binding. For Ronda's sake, he hoped she had never been mated.

So many questions; so few answers. No answers would be forthcoming until Ronda woke up from her head injury.

Swiping sweat from his forehead, Nikolas recalled the eve when he had first captured her:

He had thought her beautiful, deadly, and a liar. Beautiful and deadly had been verified, but the latter had proven false. Just as the woman he'd first thought to be a spy had claimed, an Outsider's bird *had* crashed into the mountain. A search of her clothes had revealed identification that further backed up her claim.

Now all he could do was hope, for Ronda's sake, that she settled into her new life without too much mourning for the old one.

CHAPTER FIVE

*R*onda regained semiconsciousness with a small, whimpering groan. She floated in and out of awareness, uncertain if the sound had come from her or from someone else. The pain at the side of her head had waned into a dull, barely noticeable twinge. She struggled to open her eyelids, but they felt like lead weights.

"The patient finally awakens," an old voice crooned in a thick accent. The voice was familiar. But why? "I thought I'd mayhap lost you yestereve." Her chuckle sounded more like a cackle. "Your feistiness has been the talk of the entire village. You should have known better than to stand against Lord Ericsson. Goodness, child, the warrior must outweigh you by a hundred pounds!"

Memories came flooding back. Helicopter crash. Dead crew. Underground civilization none knew existed. White slavery . . .

With much effort, Ronda forced her drug-heavy eyelids open. It took her a protracted moment and several blinks to bring the old crone she'd seen in the cavern into view.

"He probably weighs a hundred pounds more than most *men.*" She paused, her throat feeling dry and scratchy. "I'm not exactly a slim, delicate flower."

Indeed, Ronda was more on the rounded side than the beanpole side. In excellent shape, but she'd always been what her mother referred to as "voluptuous." A pretty word for chubby. Still, being "thin and in" had never much mattered to Ronda. She had been born with ample hips, a plump tush and thighs, and large breasts. That's just the way God had made her.

The old woman issued another cackle. " 'Tis an advantage down here in New Sweden to be fleshy. Warriors like a soft wife to ride after a long working day."

Ronda's cheeks pinkened. She wasn't a prude, or even shy, but she'd never heard a woman of such advanced years speak so candidly about sex. And she had no intention of being in this colony long enough to provide one of those giants with free *amoré.*

"New Sweden? This place is called New Sweden?"

"Aye. 'Tis the stronghold of New Sweden, leastways. The name of our village is Lokitown." She held up a wet cloth to Ronda's head. " 'Twas Loki, the fire god himself, who led our people to this underground enclave over a thousand years ago. And so, for Loki was the capital seat named."

Riiiiight, Ronda thought. *The fire god. These people are insane!* "Hmm, I see."

The old woman frowned. Her face could rival a basset hound's with its folds and creases. "I think you make jest of our people."

"No. No!" For some reason Ronda felt bad that she'd hurt the old woman's feelings. She was an unwilling captive, but the lady had probably been responsible for saving her life. She owed her respect if nothing else. "Well," she sighed, "maybe I was. I'm sorry. Everyone's entitled to their religious beliefs."

The old woman seemed appeased. "Soon they will become your beliefs too."

Ronda highly doubted that, but said nothing. She watched the healer tend to her head wound, gently rubbing a waxy substance into a particularly tender spot at her temple.

It slowly dawned on Ronda that her clothing had been removed. She was naked under these warm, woolly blankets. *Who* had removed her clothing? The old healer was far too weak to do so herself.

She stilled, a terrible realization jarring her. The old woman wouldn't have told her where she was and hinted that there were more such underground colonies if she didn't believe that Ronda would never escape this place.

A sinking feeling stole over her. "What will you do with me?" Ronda murmured.

The old woman sighed. "I mean you no harm, child."

"And the others?"

"It depends on what others you mean."

Ronda's eyebrows formed a golden arch over her dark gaze. "I don't understand."

"Soon you will." She stopped at her task and looked Ronda in the eyes. "I wish 'twas words of encouragement I could give to you, but so long as Toki rules here, 'tis a life of uncertainty for us all."

"I thought Toki was your god. Why would your own god harm you?"

The old woman clucked her tongue. "Loki, child. Loki, with an *L*. I speak of New Sweden's current jarl—ruler. His name is Toki, with a *T*."

"I see."

Sort of. Her head was spinning and she felt more confused than enlightened. "So what will become of me?" she softly inquired again.

The old woman's sigh was longer this time. "You will go, as all unwed females of breedable years do, to the marriage auction block. 'Twas once a place of honor and hope, a symbol of our people's continuity of life. But under Toki's regime? Bah!"

Ronda closed her eyes. Oh, God. If she didn't find a method of escape, she would end up naked on a stage in shackles, groped by men she didn't want touching her, and sold off to the highest bidder.

Her eyes flicking open, she watched the old healer wash the waxy substance from her hands under a spigot and then clean up the herbs she'd put into the potion. "Will you help me escape?" Ronda asked. A stupid question, maybe, but her only hope.

The old woman slowly shook her head. "That I cannot do."

"But—"

She held up a palm. " 'Tis not a possibility. Ever. Were

you freed, you would tell other Outsiders of our existence."
She shook her head when Ronda opened her mouth to
protest. "Not even a master as just as Lord Ericsson would
allow you to go."

The giant? If *he* was considered just, she'd hate to see
what this Toki character was like. The giant's smile while
watching her from below had been cruel, mocking, as
though he *wanted* her to be humiliated and sold to another.
He'd thought her a spy.

"He stayed with you, you know."

Ronda blinked. "I'm sorry?"

"Nikolas—Lord Ericsson," the old woman explained. "He
stayed with you and nursed you to health for most of these
past two moon-risings." She nodded. " 'Tis only for so long
that an old woman like me can stay awake and on her feet."

The giant? Somehow Ronda couldn't see him playing
nursemaid to anyone, let alone her. "Oh," she said dumbly,
unsure of what to say.

Oh, no—had *he* removed her clothing? Barely tangible
threads of memory returned in brief flickers, impressions.

A man—cradling her, cooling her fevered head, reassuring
her with his large presence. Quiet singing in a foreign
tongue—a deep, soothing voice that comforted her with
what was probably a child's lullaby. Holding her hand.
Telling her to stay strong . . .

Him?

"Rest, child," the healer said as she headed toward the
stone chamber's wooden door and knocked twice. "You'll
need it."

*　　*　　*

"Nay." Nikolas waved a dismissive hand at Old Myria. "The finest healer in all of New Sweden you may be, but a matchmaker you are not." He frowned. "I still remember the last wench you thought would make me a fine wife. Mayhap she would have, but she smelled of swine and possessed no teeth."

The old healer harrumphed. "You exaggerate. She had teeth."

"She had *one* tooth. And a half-rotted one at that."

"A person needs but one tooth, milord. 'Tis all I have left and it serves me fine."

Nikolas rolled his eyes. "You are ninety and three. She was twenty and two!" He returned his attention to the task at hand: watching the oils be bottled and prepared for the bartering stalls. This shipment he would barter in New Norway, where they were forever low on oils. 'Twould fetch him much profit in the form of more weapons. "I am busy," he grumbled. "Carry yourself to your chamber."

Myria frowned. "Thy head is thick. Niko, the girl is scared. And can you blame her? She saw her fate before being captured by you."

"And? What makes her different from the other wenches put through the same humiliating ordeal?"

"*You* captured her," she hissed. "Not Toki's henchmen. And because you captured her, milord, you can save her from being sold off to one of the jarl's sadistic soldiers."

Hunter's Right. The law was so old and sacred that not even one so daft as Toki would think to gainsay it. It decreed that whenever an unwed warrior captured a bride, he had the right to keep her for his own rather than barter her to another.

Nikolas sighed. Odin knew he was having difficulty keeping his thoughts away from the Outsider wench. She was fiery, that one. The type of woman who commanded respect. That she'd managed to thwart him once had captured his attention in a way no wench ever had before. Finding out she was indeed the innocent she'd claimed to be made her only that much more desirable. Stripping her of clothing and bathing her naked body . . .

Nikolas pinched the bridge of his nose and slowly exhaled. "Her story proved true. That much will I credit her." He turned to face the old woman. "But, Myria," he murmured so as not to be overheard, "you know the time to seize New Sweden draws near. The last thing I need is a wife to distract me from—"

"Who is to say she will distract you?"

He snorted at that. "Like as not, she will attempt to flee from me and the Underground at every turn!" He narrowed his eyes at the tiny woman who thought to change his mind. "I don't need a troublesome wife to keep in hand while I fight to overthrow the corrupt Toki." His jaw tightened. "All of our destinies are at stake here—the wench's included."

The old healer's eyes were weary with age, but sharp with wisdom. She was silent for a long moment, simply staring up at him from beneath her cowl. "You have the right," she whispered, "to know a little happiness of your own in this lifetime, Niko. Do not make every moment one where you take on the worries of the world. When you meet the gods in Valhalla, go to them having led a full life." She frowned, then clucked her tongue before wobbling away. "Think about it," she threw out over her stooped shoulders without looking back. " 'Tis all I ask."

Nikolas stared after Old Myria long after she'd trailed out of his sight. Ronda was to go up on the auction block on the morrow. Mayhap . . .

A wife? *That* wife? Nay.

He couldn't believe he'd taken the old healer's words under consideration for even the space of a breath. Even if he did wish to take advantage of Hunter's Right, a wench so beautiful of face and form might not want *him* for a husband.

Beauty was attracted to beauty—a lesson he'd learned the hard way long ago. He had been besotted with Toki's step-sister, as a boy. When he became a man and Berta had gone to the marriage auction block, he'd sought to barter for her hand in matrimony. By then Nikolas's wealth was vast and had earned him a title, so he thought he'd make her a proper husband. But each time Nikolas had raised his hand to up the ante on the previous bid, Berta had paled. Again and again and again.

"Do not permit that hideous beast to bid on me!" he'd overheard her beseech his uncle, her stepfather. "For the love of Frigga, do not allow me to be sentenced to a lifetime of being pawed at by that big, ugly hulk!"

His heart had sunk. Nikolas had quietly withdrawn from the auction, and 'twas the last time he'd sought a bride.

An overlord he might be, but Nikolas's hands were still calloused and rough, proof of his upbringing as a laborer. His body was massive—huge and heavily muscled—not the lanky, regal posturing of a man born to wealth and status. His chest was riddled with battle scars, his face rugged rather than pretty. Most wenches nigh unto swooned just looking upon him.

Nikolas blinked, his mind returning to the present. Nay, he would not claim Ronda. The wench had no choice but to remain amongst their people. She deserved a husband she could at least bear to look upon.

CHAPTER SIX

*R*onda had never been angrier or more frightened in her entire life. For the past three hours, she had been tied to a bed while various women plucked and tweezed every last pubic hair from her mons. After that, they had rubbed mint-scented oil all over her naked body—her breasts, her nipples, even her genitals.

She realized why they were doing this, of course. They were preparing her for that marriage auction block.

The thought of being forced up onto a platform as naked as the day she was born didn't sit well with her at all. She wasn't exactly embarrassed about her plump curves, but she wasn't exactly proud of them, either. She faced being sold, forced into marriage with some unknown man, and no doubt being raped by him soon thereafter—yet all she could worry about was being naked and in shackles on a platform.

She was beginning to wish she'd gone down in that chopper with the rest of the crew.

The door flew open and a man entered the chamber. His heated green gaze sought out Ronda's naked body and lingered there. " 'Tis time," the man informed them in English as he dragged his gaze away from Ronda and toward one of the women oiling her down. "Shackle her, then corral her with the others."

The women going up for sale today totaled five. One was an Inuit Eskimo who had been captured from her home, two were natives of New Sweden, one was an African-American, and then there was Ronda: the Ohio-born woman who'd gone from army corporal to sex slave in the blink of an eye.

The naked females were corralled together in a large stone pit with dim light. The two who were natives to this odd world seemed giddy with excitement, but the remaining three looked hopeless and miserable.

It wasn't like Ronda to give up so easily. And deep down inside, she knew she hadn't. But without a familiarity of the colony's layout, she had no chance of escaping.

For now there was only grim resignation. Later she would make her plans, bide her time, and escape.

"What's your name?" the African-American captive whispered. She looked as frightened as Ronda felt.

"Ronda Tipton," she replied softly. The women had been given strict orders not to speak to each other. "What about you?"

"Jonna Harper."

"It's nice to meet you."

"You too."

Ronda studied the Eskimo female for a moment, and

then Jonna. She could see why both of them had been hunted down—their beauty was exquisite. "How were you caught?" Ronda murmured.

Jonna sighed. "On a cruise ship. They took me while the boat was temporarily docked. You?"

Ronda told her about the crash.

"I want to escape," Jonna said suddenly. "Will you go with—"

The overhead door flew open, bringing their conversation to an abrupt halt.

Damn it! Just when she'd found an ally!

"Stand up and climb the steps," the auctioneer commanded in broken English. "Your future masters have gathered and await you."

Ronda couldn't believe this was happening; it still felt like a surreal dream.

"Let's go!" the auctioneer ordered. "Get off your arses and climb the steps."

The two natives of New Sweden were put up for bid first—probably to show the unwilling captives how they were expected to behave when it was their turn.

Like docile, smiling submissives.

Dozens of men had crowded into the arena to barter for a bride. The natives displayed no negative reactions whatsoever to being bodily inspected by any man that chose to touch them. They kept their heads bowed demurely, soft smiles on their faces, as large Viking males ran their hands over their breasts, over their shaved, oiled vaginas—one man was even so bold as to spread the second girl's labial lips open and flick his tongue at her clit while another man squeezed her nipples. The woman squirmed a little and sighed breathily.

If the auctioneer thought Ronda would behave like this, he had another think coming.

"Do I throw up now or later?" Jonna muttered under her breath.

Ronda snorted. "Wait and do it on whoever buys you. I'd say he deserves it."

The women shared a smile, then turned their attention back to the auction taking place.

Ronda could feel several eyes wandering over to where she, Jonna, and the other captive stood, and embarrassment stole over her. She was naked, oiled up like a bimbo at a sleazy sex bar, and shackled at the feet. Humiliation didn't come much worse than this. She'd been a POW for three weeks in Haiti and even those guards hadn't treated her like this.

The auction continued in what Ronda presumed was Swedish, or its ancient equivalent, while the two natives were bartered off. "Why isn't hardly anyone bidding on them?" she whispered to Jonna.

Jonna frowned. "I'm given to understand these assholes prefer captive brides to natives."

"Wild horses," Ronda sighed.

"Huh?"

"I've visited countries where wild horses are more valuable than domesticated ones. They're unbroken. Like unmolded clay, rather than a lump already turned into a pot or a vase. And that's exactly what we are to these crazies—wild horses."

"I'll give them a wild horse all right," Jonna muttered. "Bastards."

After the two natives were finally sold and given to their respective husbands, the auctioneer began speaking in English. The quietly crying Eskimo girl was led up to the platform. The closer she got to the throng of potential bidders, the more desperate she grew. Kicking, screaming, clawing, and hitting, it took three of the auctioneer's henchmen to forcibly subdue her.

Nostrils flaring, Ronda looked away, unable to watch. No woman should have to be treated in this fashion! If she ever escaped, she'd make sure the human rights organizations knew about this cruel place—and she would take great pleasure in doing so.

Ronda's stomach knotted and lurched when it was Jonna's turn. Though they'd only exchanged a few sentences, their conversation made it ten times harder to watch than the last auction. Jonna was a true fighter to the end. There was no such thing as subduing her. Unfortunately, that only seemed to entice buyers all the more.

One thing could be said for Jonna—nobody got any free feels out of her. Dozens of men bid on her, yet not a single one of them had gotten to so much as touch her toe. She was a wild horse for sure.

Ronda just hoped and prayed to whatever higher power was listening that the tall, muscular, blond Viking who bought her appreciated that facet of Jonna's character and didn't try to mold her into his version of what he wanted her to be. The man had made no move to grope and fondle her, and his eyes were kind. Ronda hoped that signified an overall gentleness throughout.

And then it was Ronda's turn. Her heart pounded against her chest, feeling like a heavy brick. When the auctioneer prodded her up on the platform, she made no move to kick, scream, or do anything besides stand there with a wicked *I'm gonna fuck you up* look on her face. He looked shocked.

Good.

The catcalls began. Whistles and cheers erupted as Ronda was led to center stage.

CHAPTER SEVEN

*H*olding the heavy hammer high above his head, Nikolas struck the metal with every bit of force he could muster. 'Twas the only way to block out the sounds of the auction taking place a level below. His jugular bulged and his teeth gritted from the labor.

He would *not* intervene. He had to keep reminding himself that Ronda Tipton would not care to look upon a huge, ugly beast for all of her days. Their people had carried on without intrusion from Outsiders for over a thousand years for the simple fact that none knew of their existence. Ronda was stuck in Lokitown until she took her last breath. The least that he could do was allow her to have a shot at eventual happiness.

Throwing the hammer to the side, Nikolas wiped with a rag at the sweat trickling down the side of his face.

His jaw tightened as the sounds of the marriage auction below reached his ears. His men should be up here working instead of bidding on brides! But Old Myria had encouraged his warriors to attend the event and to bid on the captives, that all might end up in honest hands. Nikolas had permitted them to do so, because he couldn't stand the idea of Ronda ending up in the clutches of a cruel master. Any bidder under Toki's regime was probably as sadistic as their leader was.

But can I stand to see her married off to one of my own men?
Nikolas sighed.

Grumbling to himself about what an idiot he was, he threw on his tunic and stalked off toward the caged lift. It couldn't hurt to see how the auction was proceeding.

Nikolas's face was the first one Ronda saw in the vast crowd of men. He was leaning against a rock wall, his arms crossed over his chest. He wore a gold chain-mail tunic today with black leather brais. The tunic was sleeveless, showcasing those massive arms clasped by gold bangles at the biceps. His dark brown hair flowed just past his shoulders, a braid at either temple tied in his trademark fashion at the back of his head.

He was the reason she was being auctioned off to begin with. Why had he come here? To remind her that he had won? To throw her another one of his mocking smiles?

The longer she watched him, though, the more she realized that wasn't the case. Nikolas wasn't making eye contact, and she couldn't tell if he was even looking at her at all. His blue eyes were hooded, his expression unreadable. He didn't look inclined to participate.

For some insane reason, that irritated Ronda. Did he think she was good enough to barter off, but not good enough to keep? Given all the obstacles between her and freedom, it might be a dumb thing to get an attitude about—but there it was.

By Odin, she was breathtaking in her beauty.

Nikolas's manhood stirred within his brais at the sight of Ronda's naked body. Mayhap 'twas wrong to lust after a wench being paraded around nude and in shackles, yet he had wanted her long before this moment. Even before the eve he'd stripped her of clothing and bathed her fevered, limp body.

He'd wanted her for his own since the moment their eyes had first met.

She had a glorious body, plump in all the right places. Her skin was light honey perfection. Her hair looked like ringlets of gold that cascaded to just above her rounded backside. Contrasted against dark, come-hither eyes, the combination was irresistible. Her breasts were mouthwateringly large with puffy pink nipples that stayed forever stiff. And her shaved pussy . . .

Nikolas took a deep breath and blew it out. He'd wanted inside her tight flesh since that first glance. He bet she'd clamp around him like an unyielding glove.

He blinked, snapping himself out of his lustful fantasies.

'Twas a certainty he would envy whatever master took her to wife.

You have the right, Myria had whispered, *to know a little happiness of your own in this lifetime, Niko. Do not make every moment one where you take on the worries of the world. When you meet the gods in Valhalla, go to them having led a full life.*

Myria's words had pounded in his heart and head since yestereve. He sighed, uncertain which was the right course to take.

More than his own happiness was at stake here. Ronda's was too.

"This, fine warriors, is Ronda!" the auctioneer cried out. Roars of approval, shouts, jests, and cheers went up like wildfire.

Ronda's dark gaze flicked to Nikolas. He wasn't laughing, cheering, or roaring. Just standing there.

"She's a fiery, spirited girl, this one. Mayhap you recall the stories about her?"

Ronda frowned at the crowd's laughter. They found it amusing that she'd put up a fight prior to capture, did they? Huh. She'd give them something to laugh about, then.

"You may approach the chattel according to rank. My lords, you have first inspection and bidding rights. Proceed!"

A hush fell over the crowd as the first high-ranking overlord made his way up to the platform. He was tall, quite gaunt and thin. Jewels were on his every finger, giving him a gaudy, somewhat feminine appearance. His hair was long and blond, his eyes green. Those eyes didn't look kind.

A smirk twisted his lips. He didn't bother to say anything, just reached out his hand toward Ronda's breasts. Down here in the rabbit hole, the rules said he had that right. Ronda had never been much for following the rules.

In a lightning-quick motion, she seized the overlord by the wrist. "Touch me," she said calmly, "and I break it."

His face turned crimson as guffaws echoed throughout the arena. A tick started in his jaw and worked its way up to his cheek. His eyes grew impossibly more sinister. "Unhand me, wench," he said, "or you *will* regret it."

Ronda held his fragile wrist for a suspended moment and squeezed, her gaze locked with his. When she felt her point had been sufficiently made, she released him.

Immediately, the idiot reached for her breast again.

True to her word, Ronda seized his wrist with her right hand. Her gaze never leaving his surprised one, she held up her left palm in a karate move and struck.

His wrist snapped like a chicken bone. He cried out in pain, falling to his knees.

And all hell broke loose.

"Subdue the bitch!"

Two of the auctioneer's guards responded to their overseer's cry.

When Ronda had broken the sadistic Nothrum's wrist, admiration and pleasure had glinted in Nikolas's eyes. Now he tensed as he watched the two henchmen approach her.

Her feet were shackled. What could the wee, defenseless wench do? The guards were big and brawny, 'twas an unfair match. Enraged, he started toward the platform.

In a movement so fast it seemed inhuman, Ronda flipped over into a handstand, her palms on the platform's dirt floor, and scissored her legs. On a guttural "Hiya!" sound, she uncrossed them with enough brute force to break both of her ankles.

The shackles snapped instead.

Total silence engulfed the arena. "Holy son of Odin." Nikolas's jaw went slack, his eyes unblinking.

The first guard bellowed as he charged her.

Ronda countered with a jump in the air that was high enough to make the crowd gasp. She whirled around midair and kicked the guard's face in six pummeling strikes that sent him flying onto his back. When he slowly regrouped and came up to his knees, she kicked him again, this time square in the face, breaking his nose.

Seizing the crowd's shock to her advantage, she jumped down from the platform and ran—but her victory was short-lived. Where one or two men could not subdue her, ten could. And it took about that many to get the job done.

As Nikolas roughly pushed through the crowd to get to her, Ronda's eyes found his—wild, desperate, and pleading. It all but broke his heart. There was nothing weak about this woman.

As the guards and a few of Toki's men took her down to the ground, Nikolas ruthlessly shoved others aside and finally reached Ronda. They had her facedown, her wrists and feet being tied behind her back. One man laughed and reached out to stroke her buttocks, and Nikolas erupted in rage.

Roaring, he flung Toki's trusted overlords off Ronda. The other men immediately backed away. All stunned eyes turned to him.

"Hunter's Right!" Nikolas bellowed, his lethal stance defying any man to approach him. The vein at his neck bulged. "I claim her for my own! Does any warrior here dare challenge me?"

Silence followed the echo of his booming voice from the arena's walls. Nikolas's angry stare sought out Nothrum who had enough sense to look away. 'Twas a good thing, for Nikolas's fury was powerful enough to kill any man who tried him.

His eyes narrowing into menacing blue slits, Nikolas turned his attention to the men near Ronda who sat gawking up at him.

"Lämna min fru i fred," he said quietly.

The men scattered. Wasting no time, Nikolas knelt and began untying the knots that held Ronda painfully bound.

"What did you say to them?" Ronda whispered, her scared brown eyes wide.

"I told them," Nikolas said as he continued undoing the knots, "to get away from my wife."

Ronda Tipton was married.

She'd spoken no words of commitment, given no pledge of love and devotion, yet by the laws of New Sweden she was now the legal wife of Lord Nikolas Ericsson. Just like that. She was so stunned that she didn't say a word as he slipped his tunic over her head to cover her body.

Then she followed quietly and without protest as Nikolas took her by the hand and led her from the arena.

CHAPTER EIGHT

One week later

$\mathcal{R}$onda lay in her bed way past the time when she would normally get up and start the day. So much was on her mind, so many questions, that she didn't have the energy to force herself up from the animal hides.

She had been Nikolas's wife for a week now. His wife! More shocking still was that she'd barely seen him since the night of the auction. He'd made few attempts to even talk to her, let alone touch her.

The night of the auction still seemed a daze. She remembered her captor-turned-savior slipping his tunic over her head and leading her away from the arena. She recalled not speaking as they'd entered the caged elevator and taken it down thirteen levels to where his surprisingly lavish home was. Misleadingly small on the outside, it was palatial on the inside. With all the silk pillows and harem-style beds, it brought to mind the home of a medieval sultan. Most of the rooms even had several skylights, allowing the sun to penetrate during daylight hours. That certainly explained Nikolas's bronzed body and how the people remained in good health despite living below the ground.

Ronda had expected Nikolas to rape her, for Myria had warned her that warriors consummated their marriages on the evening they became wedded. That had not happened. In fact, he'd been surprisingly gentle and understanding as he gave her a tour of what he called "our dwelling." He explained that she was free to roam its rooms and make use of them, but asked her not to leave the home without his escort because it wouldn't be safe to do so.

Escape, he had told her, was impossible. Armed guards lined every possible way out of New Sweden, and now, since she'd stumbled upon their world by accident, they were also positioned at the upper level of the mountain.

After that quiet lecture, he'd escorted her into this bedchamber, told her it belonged to her, and bid her goodnight. That had been the most he'd spoken to her at one time in over a week. In fact, that had been the most she'd seen of him all week. He'd spent most of his time away from the dwelling, while Ronda stayed in her bedchamber, grieving the loss of freedom she'd once taken for granted.

Ronda sighed. Now she was growing bored and lonely. Other than the two servants who cajoled her into eating a few times daily and who had finally got her to enter the dwelling's bathing pond yesterday so they could scrub her down, keep her mons shaved, and rub mint oil into her skin, she didn't really have any contact with anyone.

That bath had been more embarrassing than relaxing.

Bathing with two naked female servants was something she'd never before done.

Other than maid one and maid two, both of whom spoke no English, there was nobody to talk to. She couldn't take much more of this sitting in isolation, nor could she endure any more grieving for what would never again be.

Ronda was a realist. Common sense dictated that these underground dwellers had never been discovered in over a thousand years because they guarded their turf with an iron fist. Which didn't bode well for escape. Not now and not ever.

That left two choices: try to escape at every turn and grow more depressed, if not dead, from lack of success, or try to carve out some sort of meaningful life for herself down here. It had taken her a solid week to arrive at this conclusion, but she'd finally gotten to where she needed to be, mentally speaking.

In that way, she was glad Nikolas had left her alone these past seven days. It had given her time to cry over the freedom she'd lost, come to terms with the situation for what it was, and make a profound choice. Ronda had decided that she wanted to find some kind of happiness, even if that came at the price of living out the rest of her life in Loki-town.

But what about Nikolas? What had he given up to save her? For the first time, Ronda found her thoughts turning to his predicament rather than her own.

Did he have a love he'd wanted to marry, but had wedded Ronda out of some sense of duty to protect her? Had he given up someone special? *Why* had he claimed her for his own?

She could easily see any number of women falling for Nikolas. He was not only politically powerful in this underground world, but he was also handsome as sin. With the body of a well-honed warrior and the ruggedly masculine face of an avenging god, no woman from Ronda's world wouldn't worship at his feet.

So many questions. So few answers.

Ronda forced the heavy animal hides off her body. Taking a deep, cathartic breath, she decided it was time to rejoin the living.

Nikolas studied his logbook, his mind distracted. He needed to concentrate on determining how many bottles of oils were ready for bartering in New Norway, yet his thoughts kept returning to his wife.

He wondered if she'd ever remove herself from the guest bedchamber—now *her* bedchamber—and at least attempt to have peace between them. Nikolas had left her alone this past week when he'd wanted to do anything but that. Talk with her, eat with her, make love to her. Anything but leave her alone.

Still, he recognized that she needed time to settle into the way of things. He could well imagine the myriad emotions he'd be experiencing were their roles here reversed. 'Twould be difficult at best and mayhap impossible to accept that he'd never again lay eyes on all that was familiar to him.

He sighed, hoping such would not be the case with

Ronda. He found himself praying to the gods more oft than usual, focusing on his wife. Prayers of a peace between them. And mayhap, if he was lucky, even an eventual love.

When Otrygg loudly barged into the den, Nikolas glanced up. The older, fuming warrior was accompanied by his thirty-three-year-old, equally irate nephew, Erikk.

"You will not believe this, milord," Otrygg bit out.

"He's a perverter of the law," Erikk chimed in.

Nikolas raised an eyebrow. "Toki? One of his regime?" He frowned. "And speak in English. Toki and his idiot imbeciles never learned it."

Otrygg's face was beet red with his fury. He was so worked up that it took him a moment to get his words out. He did, however, switch the conversation to the Outsider tongue. "Toki is forcing my sister, Froda, to the auction block."

Nikolas stilled. " 'Tis impossible. She—"

" 'Tis true, milord," Erikk said bitterly. "Toki's soldiers came to my mother's dwelling last eve. They gave her a fortnight to say good-bye to her old life and prepare for her new one."

"But she's a widow," Nikolas said, stunned. "And a widow beyond childbearing years, at that."

"Nothrum covets her," Otrygg informed him. "The sadistic little bastard always has. And what Nothrum wants, Toki gives him."

Nikolas stood up. For as long as the Underground had existed, widows of all clans in all three kingdoms—New Sweden, New Norway, and New Daneland—had enjoyed a protected, sacred status. 'Twas up to them if they wished to remarry or even dally with another warrior once their husbands left this realm to join the gods and goddesses in Valhalla.

"The time to take New Sweden is *now*," Nikolas said quietly but forcefully. The agreed-upon date for the coup was still a month off, but the seizing of power couldn't wait. "Already public opinion sways to our side. When word of this spreads throughout the colony, chaos might very well reign!"

"Agreed. This is about more than my mother, milord. This is about the stability and sanctity of our entire way of life. All families will fear that their matriarch will be taken from them." Erikk's nostrils flared. "If you are prepared to lead, then I am prepared to fight."

The two warriors locked eyes and Nikolas nodded. To save Erikk's mother from Nothrum's vile hands, the time to overthrow Toki's regime was coming upon them in a mere fourteen days. There was much preparation to do.

"Maintain control here whilst I voyage to New Norway with some of my men to barter for more weapons. Can you do that?" Nikolas waited for both uncle and nephew to nod their agreement before continuing. "Call upon the three elders we know to be loyal to Toki's dead sire and the impending coup. Round them up and tell them in secrecy what is to become of Froda. Tell them *not* to tell anyone in Lokitown yet."

Lord Ericsson continued to pace. "Instruct them to ready their nobles—all of them from all five of our clans. Lokitown is positioned at the middle of New Sweden, so besieging from without as well as from within is key."

" 'Tis also important that word of the coup not spread to the New Norwegians or the New Danes," Otrygg added. "They would seize the opportunity to envelop New Sweden while she's vulnerable."

Nikolas agreed. "Other than my first in command, I won't even tell my men why the urgency behind this voyage."

"You will win, milord," Erikk murmured. "And, at last, you will be our king."

"The balance of power has been shifting to your side in greater numbers these past several months. I stand behind your decision that this is the time," Otrygg affirmed. "I hereby pledge my life and loyalty to you and your house."

"As do I." Erikk inclined his head.

Nikolas had waited many moon-risings to hear those words from Otrygg's lips. The elder warrior was wise and experienced. He had known the time for the coup would be right when at last Otrygg had given him his oath.

"I thank you." Blinking, Nikolas cleared his throat. "And now I must ask you to leave me, that I might get the voyage to New Norway in progress with all speed."

Otrygg patted him on the back. "Who will you take with you, Niko?"

"I would like to go."

The men stilled. All gazes flew toward the entrance of the den.

Ronda?

Nikolas's heartbeat had picked up at the mere sound of her voice. Looking upon her, dressed in the nearly see-through silk tunic of their people's women, no less, damn near made his heart beat out of his chest.

She looked utterly breathtaking in a blue tunic that began just at the cleavage line and draped to her ankles. The gold rope that crisscrossed at her hips kept the hemline from falling to her toes. The elastic band that circled the entire upper portion kept her breasts from spilling out of the sleeveless, slinky slip of a dress. Her stiff nipples poked against the sheer material of the tunic.

Nikolas blew out a breath. The gown offered no protection from his lust, and he had the achingly swollen erection to prove it.

"I'm an excellent strategist."

Nikolas forced his gaze away from her body and up to her face. Not that it helped matters much. Her features were so strikingly exotic in their beauty that he stayed hard anyway. "I'm sorry?" he said, snapping out of the fantasy that involved riding her for about twenty-four solid hours.

"Above the ground, that's part of what I did during times of war—strategize. I decided how many troops would go where and allocated the necessary funds to see it through."

She had been a warrior in her world. In his lust, such knowledge had temporarily been forgotten. "I see."

Ronda sighed. "I can take care of myself, if you're worried I'll get in the way."

Of that Nikolas held no doubts. Never had he seen a woman—or a man for that matter—break shackles made from iron with just the crossing and uncrossing of her legs. And the high jump in the air with the series of kicks? Any potential attackers would swoon. Verily, Nikolas was the only warrior he knew with a fearsome wife. 'Twas odd, but in a pleasant way that filled him with pride. "It isn't that, so much, as I'm certain you would not care to step foot in New Norway."

Otrygg chuckled. "Mayhap you should let her go, milord. Like as not, New Sweden will seem a paradise in contrast."

"What do you mean?" Ronda asked, glancing over to the older warrior.

"Let us just say," Erikk interjected, gaining him her attention, "that the lot in life for the wenches of New Norway is considered barbaric by our people."

Ronda's eyes widened. She couldn't imagine a place that treated women with even less respect than this one. She was currently dressed like a sex kitten, she held no true political rights, was supposed to call her husband "master," and was taken to task by the female servants at every meal for not sleeping with her master and seeing to his manly needs. They might not speak English, but she had no problem translating the irate lectures—mainly because a lot of it revolved around pointing toward Nikolas's bedroom and shaking their heads at her.

"Worse than this place?" Ronda shook her head. "What do they do to them? Put apples on their heads and use them for target practice with a bow and arrow?"

That got a laugh out of the three men. Ronda's heart stilled. She'd never seen Nikolas wear a genuine smile before, and it suited him . . . better than perfectly. He even had a hint of a dimple.

"Not so bad as that," Nikolas said, a twinkle in his eyes.

"Then I can handle it."

"I don't think it's a good idea." Nikolas's smile dissolved. "The Underground waterways are often treacherous. And when we arrive in New Norway, you will be expected to dress as their women do. And—"

Ronda held up a palm. "I'm not the type of woman who can just sit around all day and sew, okay?" And she highly doubted their manner of dress could be much worse than the ensemble she was currently wearing! She felt like the Queen of the Slut People. "If you want us to move forward together, then you've got to respect that."

Nikolas's heart thumped in his chest. She was hinting at a truce. Mayhap even more.

"I'd really like to go, Nikolas. Please."

He sighed, then said, "Have the servants prepare you a satchel of clothing." He really had to stop this business of acting the in-love milksop whenever she was near. Frowning, he began walking away. "We leave within the hour."

CHAPTER NINE

*T*rue to his word, they left within the hour. And Ronda got to see more of the underworld kingdom.

The longboat they boarded looked like classic Viking handiwork straight out of antiquity, but on a smaller scale. Nikolas had told her that they were preparing to travel through a man-made underground waterway that was only big enough for two boats to pass each other simultaneously.

The lower deck contained two sleeping chambers, a crude kitchen, and a common area. The upper deck featured six fixed oars that warriors manually maneuvered—three on each side—and two rows of chairs in the middle.

Nikolas put a cloak around Ronda's shoulders. "There's a chill in the air this far below, so I don't advise removing it."

She nodded, already feeling goose bumps. "Yes, I feel it."

He smiled, then helped her to her seat aboard the longboat.

Six imposing Viking warriors, each wearing a hooded black robe, were already in position at the oars. They reminded her of the boatman on the fabled river Styx. "The bottled oils are already loaded?" she quietly inquired, settling in next to Nikolas.

"Aye. My men move quickly."

"Huh. *You* sure don't. I-I mean . . ." Her eyes rounded. Ronda couldn't believe what she'd just said! The words had stumbled out of her mouth without her thinking about them; she just hoped he hadn't caught the double entendre.

"I had the boat ready within an hour. Why would you call me slow?"

She frowned. He *hadn't* caught the double entendre. She didn't know whether to be frustrated or relieved.

"I was joking. Where did you learn English?" *Obviously your tutors neglected to teach the delicate art of reading between the lines!*

Okay, she sniffed, so she was frustrated. She blamed her raging hormones on her not having had sex since bright pink lipstick and gaudy blue eye-shadow had been in vogue.

And on the way Nikolas had been staring at her through heavy eyelids in his den.

"Most men of the laboring class know how to speak it. A way to have one up on the overlords, I suppose." He shrugged. "My English is simply different from yours. Every people possess their own dialect."

"How did you learn it, if it's the second tongue of laborers? I thought you were an overlord."

Ronda could have sworn she felt him tense up beside her.

"I was not born within the class of nobles," Nikolas said softly. "I was born the second son of a fifth son. 'Tis a long, complicated, and boring tale. Suffice it to say I grew up amongst the laborers."

"You worked your way up in the ranks instead of inheriting it?"

Again, the tensing. "Aye."

Ronda smiled as she found his gaze. "That's very cool."

"Cool?"

"Yeah, cool. You know—umm . . . sort of a cross between admirable and desirable."

Silence. His eyelids grew heavy again as their gazes held. "I think you are cool too," he murmured.

She couldn't help it. She had to grin. The way he had said it was just too cute. Her eyes sparkled as she held his stare. Reaching up to his face, she tucked a lock of hair behind one of his ears. "Thank you," she whispered back.

They reverted to silence as the boat took off. Ten men at the rear who were standing on the dock gave it a push. Within seconds of hitting the water, the longboat neared a ramp. The oarsmen began rowing, heading toward a dark tunnel.

"Hold on!" one of the men called out. "Here we go!"

Ronda yelped as the longboat went racing downhill like a water ride in an amusement park. She instinctively reached for Nikolas's hand to steady herself. Laughing, she glanced up at her husband.

"This is cool?" He smiled.

"Yeah! But in a different way!"

The longboat raced downhill for thirty seconds more before the waterway evened out and turned flat. The oarsmen then returned to rowing and steering the vessel toward their destination.

An hour later, Ronda was yawning. Two hours later and she could barely keep her eyes open. "How much longer until we get there?" she asked Nikolas.

"Another ten hours or so."

"Ten hours? Good grief! I had no idea the Underground was so vast."

His blue gaze flicked over her features. "Why do you not go below and get some rest? There won't be much to see beyond tunnels for another seven hours or so."

Silence.

"What about you?" Ronda finally asked, her voice soft. "Don't you need some rest too?"

If he missed this double entendre, she'd have to write him a book called *Reading Between the Lines 101*.

"I'm not overly tired."

Somebody get me a typewriter!

"Nikolas," Ronda sighed. She ran a hand through her blond curls. "I really don't want to be alone down there."

Again, silence.

"Mayhap 'twould be, uh, cool . . . if I lie beside you?"

"Very cool." She smiled.

The lower deck was lit up by lightbulbs on wall sconces— something she'd noticed in their dwelling, as well. "I see you've discovered Thomas Edison in New Sweden."

"Thomas Edison?" Nikolas inquired as he led her toward the bedchamber.

"Yes." Ronda pointed up at one of the lights as they passed by it. "The guy who invented lightbulbs in the year 1879."

Nikolas sniffed at that. "Our people have had the bulbs you speak of since 1622. 'Twas invented by Milo Torgysson."

"No kidding?"

He grunted his acknowledgment. "Aye."

The bedchamber turned out to be quite cramped and sparse. Then again, there wouldn't be much need for lavishness on a longboat. The warriors didn't spend months on them sailing the oceans, only a couple of days here and there on the underground waterways.

Taking a deep breath, Ronda removed her cloak and worked up her nerve. She had spent an entire week thinking and rethinking things, changing her opinions again and again, until she had at last made up her mind on how life would be from here on out. Once she made up her mind, she didn't change it. It was just the way she was and had always been: stubborn and steadfast to the bone.

She wanted to carve out a meaningful, happy life for herself. She didn't want to spend any more time brooding over what could have been. She realized that Nikolas would never let her go—he couldn't. And it was not as if her life had been all that exhilarating prior to her capture. She'd asked for some excitement in her life, and she'd gotten it. In spades. Whatever the circumstances leading up to her marriage, it was time to accept that she was indeed married.

"Soooo," Ronda said, her cheeks pinkening a little as she

stood on one side of the bed, her husband on the other. "What do your people wear when they go to sleep?"

Nikolas stilled. "Nothing."

She blew out a breath. Finally they were getting somewhere. She'd never tried seducing a man before; usually it was the other way around. The role of seducer was difficult. You could never be totally sure if the other party wanted you or would reject you.

"But I understand if you wish to sleep in your tunic. 'Tis cold down here."

Ronda sighed. How was *that* to be interpreted? Either he didn't want her or he was letting her set the pace. Unfortunately, there was only one way to find out the answer.

Slipping out of her sandals and undoing the gold rope at her waist, Ronda kept her eyes lowered to the ground. "In your world," she whispered, lifting the tunic dress over her head and tossing it aside, "what does a beautiful woman look like?" She'd never felt so vulnerable in her life, standing totally naked in front of a man, eyes downcast rather than courageous, and basically asking him if he liked what he saw.

"Like you," he said thickly. Her gaze flicked up. "Leastways, they aspire to. I've never seen a woman so beautiful as you."

His blue eyes were heavy-lidded as he studied every curve of her body. His gaze lingered at her shaved mons before roaming up to her breasts. "And I've never seen nipples that look so ripe."

Her heart thumped. "Is that why you picked me?" she murmured, the dampness between her thighs increasing.

His gaze flicked up to her face. "Nay."

She blinked. "Then why?"

"Because," Nikolas said softly, "you are full of fire and life. I couldn't bear to see one of those men break you and extinguish all that you are."

Ronda's gaze wandered over his face, memorized it. "That's the most beautiful thing anyone has ever said to me." She drew in a shaky breath. Uncharacteristically, she felt the beginnings of tears welling up in her eyes. She quickly batted them away. "Thank you."

He was quiet for a moment, then began undressing. He removed first his tunic, next his boots, and finally his brais. Ronda's breathing grew heavy as she watched him bare that hard, honed warrior's body to her eyes. By the time his long, thick erection sprang loose from the brais, desire had coiled tightly in her belly.

"The men of your world? What is handsome up there?"

It took her a moment to respond; she was too busy staring. "They want to look like you," she said honestly, her gaze flicking from that huge erection to his face, "but few ever achieve it."

His face colored a bit. On a giant warlord like Nikolas, the effect was oddly charming. "You lie," he muttered.

Her eyes widened. Was he serious? Good grief! "I don't lie." Her forehead wrinkled. "What is handsome on a man down here?"

He shrugged. "Nothrum. The man whose wrist you broke."

"*Ewwww!* He's pale and skinny and looks more like a woman than a man. Where I come from, women like men to be big and strong and sexy. Like you."

"You think me sexy?" he asked hoarsely.

Ronda wet her lips as their gazes clashed. In her world, she was considered average. Down here, she was beautiful. In his world, he was considered average. Up there, he was handsome. They were two vulnerable peas in their own little pod. "Very," she whispered.

"Is that why you picked me? Why your eyes sought me out at the auction?"

"Yes."

Nikolas grinned. God, he had a great grin. "I can live with that."

Her smile faded, and she said seriously, "But it wasn't the only reason."

"The other?"

"I knew you'd never let anybody hurt me."

Silence.

"If you get on that bed," Nikolas said thickly, his eyes intense, "there is no going back. I have but so much willpower."

Ronda dove for the bed. Nikolas threw his head back and laughed. She grinned up at him, then spread her legs wide open. His smile dissolved, replaced with heavy breathing and pre-cum dripping from the tip of his swollen cock.

God, he was gorgeous. Deadly body. Rugged masculine beauty. All primal, lethal male.

Never in her entire life had she wanted a man with the fire that she craved Nikolas.

Nikolas's breathing grew harsh as he watched his gorgeous wife spread open her bald nether lips and massage her tiny little clit. Her head fell back against the pillows on a moan as her plump nipples jutted into the air.

He'd wanted her since the first moment he'd laid eyes on her. Suppressing his desire had grown increasingly more difficult with each moment. Every second a new fantasy of what he wanted to do to Ronda had forced its way into his mind. Thank the gods he no longer had to squelch his appetite.

Nikolas dove between his wife's legs, removed her hands from her wet, musky-scented flesh, and replaced them with his hungry mouth. She gasped, her hips instinctively rearing up, her fingers twining through his hair as he sucked long and hard on her delicious pussy.

"Oh, God," Ronda moaned, wrapping her legs around his neck. Her teeth gritting, she used her hands to press his face as close to her flesh as humanly possible. "Oh, yes," she ground out, her hips undulating back and forth. "Eat it, Nikolas. Oh, God—oh, yes!—*eat me.*"

Nikolas suckled harder. She moaned, her lower body shaking as she prepared to come.

He sucked harder. And harder and harder and harder.

"Oh, God! Oh, yes! Ohhhhh, Godddddd!"

She came on a loud scream, convulsing as she gave him a violent orgasm.

He growled low in his throat. She tasted so good. She tasted like . . . his.

"Oh, Nikolas," Ronda murmured as her breathing began returning to normal. "Mmmm."

He gave her flesh one last hard suck, then released it.

When he lifted his face from between her thighs, he noticed that her eyes were closed, a dreamy smile on her face.

He also noticed those hard, pink nipples that he'd been dying to taste.

Settling himself intimately between her legs, Nikolas palmed both breasts in his warrior-calloused hands. He pushed her large breasts together as closely as they would go, then dined.

He flicked at and sucked on her stiff nipples one at a time, going from one to the other and back again. Ronda whimpered, lifting her bottom up so that her female flesh pressed against his hard stomach. She wanted him inside her, but he took his time, sucking on those nipples the way he'd often fantasized doing while stroking his big cock and pretending she wanted him as much as he wanted her.

"Nikolas," she groaned in a pleading voice, her body writhing under his, *"please* fuck me. *I'm begging you."*

He released one of her nipples with a popping sound, his head lifting from her breasts. Grabbing his thick erection by the root, he pressed the swollen tip against her opening. "Is this what you want?" he murmured, his eyelids heavy.

"Yes," she panted.

How often he'd dreamed of watching her lie beneath him, begging to be fucked by him. Strong, feisty, gorgeous, and determined—all that he'd ever wanted, all that he'd never believed he'd have.

Now he had her. And he would never let go.

"Tell me," he whispered, his gaze drugged with passion.

He pressed the head of his cock a bit farther into her tight, gripping pussy. "Tell me how bad you want me."

"Real bad," she ground out. "Nikolas, *please!"*

Ronda felt that she'd go insane if he didn't impale her right now. The thought of reversing their positions and taking what she wanted crossed her mind, but he outweighed her by a solid hundred pounds. This man was 250 pounds of honed muscle.

"Give it to me," she hissed. *"Pleeeeeease."*

"Admit that you are mine." His jaw tightened. "Vow to me that you will never lie with another."

"I swear it. I'm yours! *Nikolas* . . . I need you to—"

Ronda gasped as he entered her flesh to the hilt in one long stroke. Her eyes watered a bit at the invasion, as it had been a long time since she'd had sex. And she'd never had sex with a man as large as Nikolas.

"You feel so good," he said hoarsely, his eyelids impossibly heavier. "I love how tight and wet *my* wife is."

She loved the way he'd emphasized *my.* It spoke to some primitive need for protection that had been imprinted by cave ancestors, even though she could take care of herself just fine.

Nikolas began to thrust in and out of her, long, possessive strokes that made her moan. "And I love the way you feel inside me," Ronda breathed out, her aching nipples poking up against his chest. "So thick and powerful and filling."

He took her harder, rocking in and out of her gripping flesh while they clung to each other and groaned out their passion for the other. The intoxicating scent of their combined sweat and arousal filled the air.

"Harder," she ground out. "Give it to me real hard."

"Like this?" He pounded inside her deep and fast. Her breasts jiggled with every thrust. "Mmmm, you feel so good."

"Oh, God—I want to come!"

In a lightning-quick movement, Nikolas came up to his knees and threw Ronda's legs over his shoulders. Pressing on her clit with his thumb, he impaled her over and over and over as she moaned, writhed, and threw her hips back at him.

He rode her hard, mercilessly pumping in and out of her flesh. Ronda gasped as the tingle in her clit coiled tight.

The sound of slick skin slapping against slick skin, her sex sucking back in his cock, the pressure of his thumb at her clit—

"Oh. My. God—Nikolaaaaaaas!"

She came hard, groaning as a violent orgasm washed over her. Blood rushed to her face, heating it. Blood rushed to her nipples, elongating them. She bucked harder, wanting him to experience the same pleasure he'd just given to her.

"Ronda." His jaw was tense, his jugular bulging. He fucked her harder, slamming in and out of her. Once, twice, three times more . . .

Nikolas came on a loud growl, his teeth gritting as his body convulsed. She kept pushing her hips up at him, milking him for every bit of juice he had to give. He groaned out his praise, loving every second of it. She didn't stop until, spent, he collapsed on top of her.

They lay there, holding each other, clinging to each other, in comfortable silence. It was a long while before their breathing returned to normal.

Nikolas got up from the bed only long enough to fetch some animal hides. When he returned to the bed, Ronda snuggled up with him beneath the furs. She rested her head on his chest as his vein-roped arm came around her, holding her close to him.

"It occurs to me," he murmured, "that we still haven't kissed."

She smiled from where her head lay on his chest. "So kiss me already," she whispered.

He wasted no time in meeting her challenge. Nikolas kissed her as she'd never been kissed before.

And made her heart ache for him in a way that, on the day of her capture, she hadn't thought would ever be possible.

CHAPTER TEN

*O*trygg had been correct about one thing: in contrast New Norway *did* make New Sweden seem like a women's rights paradise. At least in Lokitown, Ronda had been permitted to wear clothing.

"Nikolas," Ronda gritted out, "please don't tell me these people actually expect me to take off my dress while we have dinner with them."

He sighed. "Did I not try to warn you before we departed?"

Yes, he had. And she had refused to listen to his arguments pertaining to why she should remain behind. *Arrrrg!*

"'Twill be but two hours at most," he said to comfort her. For whatever comfort that offered! "Only whilst the warriors unload the oils and load the bartered weapons."

She sighed, then pinched the bridge of her nose. "Are you sure they won't let me keep on my clothes?" she asked hopefully. "Maybe since I don't live here, they won't expect me to abide by their—"

"We expect them to obey our laws when in New Sweden."

Ronda frowned, but conceded the point. "Okay." Damn it! There didn't seem to be a graceful way out of this. If she refused to remove her clothing, she was a lawbreaker. If she remained on the boat, she'd not only be in the warriors' way, but would also be considered terminally rude. "Only for two hours?" she miserably retorted, sounding every inch the martyr she felt to be.

He nodded. "We will be on our way back to Lokitown before you know it."

It was the longest two hours of Ronda's thirty-three-year-old life. Not only were the females of New Norway's Hallfreor clan forbade clothing, but they were regarded as little more than slaves by these war-hungry men.

Nikolas had told her that the custom of the marriage auction block had come to New Sweden via the New Danes. But it was from New Norway that Toki had copied the selling of naked women who could be poked at by any lust-hungry warrior with bartering rights. If Lord Ericsson successfully overthrew Toki's regime, he planned to revert to the old way. Ronda had no idea what the "old way" consisted of, but just about anything would be better than the status quo.

As guests of the Hallfreor's ruling noble, they ate within his large, lavish dwelling at the docks. Ronda was the only female permitted at the table. The others, all as naked as she was, were either serving food or attending to their master.

This particular noble clearly enjoyed having several

nude, subservient women around him at all times, their at-
tentions devoted exclusively to him. They sat at his feet
gazing worshipfully up at him, not so much as blinking
unless he motioned for them to do this or that. Occasion-
ally he would reach down and stroke one of them or play
with another one's nipples. It brought to mind a man petting his cats.

Do I throw up now or later?

As Ronda recalled Jonna's words, she wondered how the
beautiful woman was settling into life in New Sweden.
When they returned to Lokitown, she would ask to see her.

The noble's eyes kept flicking to Ronda's naked breasts,
the only part of her he could see while seated at the table.
Her only consolation was that Nikolas clearly didn't care for
it, either. He had a possessive arm clamped around Ronda,
letting everyone in the dining chamber know just whom she
belonged to.

Aboveground, she hadn't liked possessiveness in a man.
Below the ground, it was not only welcome, but seemed to
be a necessity to keep from being manhandled or worse.

"I would be willing to barter extra weapons," the lord of
the Hallfreor clan announced, his gaze darting from Ronda's
nipples to Nikolas's face, "if you would be willing to part
with some of your balls of light."

"Balls of light?" Nikolas asked, an eyebrow arching.

"Aye. Those concoctions you have that contain fire in a
ball."

Lightbulbs, Ronda thought. Apparently the New Swedes
hadn't shared Milo's invention with the two other Under-

ground kingdoms. That explained why they were eating by torchlight—not that she was complaining: it made it more difficult for the oversexed noble to discern her nude body.

"I believe we have a few cartons aboard ship. I can leave two of those cartons behind . . . for the right price."

"And that price would be?"

"Ten more guns and fifteen more swords."

Lord Hallfreor hesitated only briefly before inclining his head. " 'Tis done."

The remainder of the meal passed by mercifully fast. Now that Lord Pervert was concentrating on bartering with Nikolas, Ronda felt more relaxed. In fact she ended up rather enjoying the meal, for the great food.

Before she knew it, it was time to reboard the longboat and sail back to Lokitown. Ronda thanked the noble for his hospitality as she stood up, and the man's gaze lowered to her bald mons.

"And I thank you too," Nikolas growled, flying to his feet. His blue gaze was as icy as when Ronda had first seen it. "We shall depart for New Sweden anon."

"Come now, old friend. Why not stay the moon-rising?" A glimmer of amusement, and recognition of Nikolas's jealousy, sparked in the noble's eyes.

A tic formed in Lord Ericsson's jaw. "Nay. We prefer to return home."

As soon as they boarded the longboat, Ronda made a beeline for the bedchamber to retrieve her tunic-dress. One thing was certain: she'd never be asking her husband to take her on a vacation to New Norway. Nooooo thank you! Clothing was her friend, a new mantra.

Bent over the bed as she searched for the garment, she was so busy throwing animal hides this way and that, that she didn't hear Nikolas enter the bedchamber.

Two strong, calloused hands seized her hips from behind, making her gasp in momentary fright. His long, thick cock slid into her gripping flesh all the way, turning her gasp into a moan. "Nikolas," she breathed out, glancing over her shoulder.

His territorial stare looked more animal than human, his muscles tense and ready to take her. He was still fully dressed, his brais down just enough to let his erect cock and tight balls spring free.

"You're mine," he ground out, deeply impaling her again. "All mine."

"Yes," Ronda panted, falling onto the bed and lifting her buttocks high in the air. "I am."

Palming both round cheeks in his hands, Nikolas wasted no time in branding her body as his possession. He rode her without mercy, sinking into her aroused flesh again and again. Ronda's large breasts jiggled beneath her with each of his thrusts, her nipples getting stiff and aroused.

"Harder," she gasped. *"More."*

"Do you like my cock buried inside you?" His voice was forceful and laced with more than a little jealousy. His thrusts came harder, faster, deeper. *"Do you?"*

"Yes," Ronda groaned, pushing her hips back at him, meeting him thrust for thrust. "I love your cock."

He went primal on her then, plunging in and out of her so hard, deep, and fast that all she could do was scream and come—twice. Nikolas's body tensed up after her second orgasm, his breathing labored, his moans telling her without words that he was ready to burst.

He came inside her on a loud roar, pumping frenetically as he emptied his seed inside her tight flesh. She threw her hips back at him—faster! faster! faster!—loving the sound of his animalistic groan while she milked his cock of its sperm.

By the time they finished, Ronda was so exhausted that it was all she could do to crawl to the middle of the bed, where, panting as if she'd just run a marathon, she collapsed. Nikolas chuckled, then fell to the bed beside her, his breathing just as heavy.

Within moments they were under the animal hides again, snuggling as they had before. Nikolas stroked her hair as she laid her head on his chest.

"I don't know what hand fate will deal me when we return to Lokitown and I declare war on the jarl." Nikolas squeezed her tightly. "Just know that I will die to protect you, and that even should I go to the gods in Valhalla, you will dwell in my heart forever."

Tears stung Ronda's eyes. "I won't let you die," she vowed. "Never."

His smile was soft, gentle—an expression at total odds with the rough, rugged warlord wearing it. "I believe you." He was quiet for a moment, then: "Should I live to defeat Toki . . ."

"Yes?"

"Do you think that . . . mayhap . . ." His gaze searched hers. "Do you think that mayhap one day you might grow to love me?"

Ronda's lips curved into a smile. "I think we're already heading that way fast, Nikolas Ericsson," she whispered. "Very fast."

"As do I." His lips found hers. "As do I," he murmured against them.

EPILOGUE

Twenty years later

*I*t hadn't taken Ronda Ericsson long at all to fall in love with her husband. Indeed, she sometimes wondered if she hadn't loved him from the moment he'd saved her at the auction. He had proven then what he'd proved time and time again over the years—Nikolas's heart was true, his love loyal, and his protection a given. Ronda had learned a lot about what love really meant over the past two decades.

Not that she hadn't taught her warlord husband plenty herself. She'd instructed him in the art of karate and, more important, in the understanding that he was worthy of being loved. He had been a king for almost as long as they'd been married, but her feelings for him would have been the same if he weren't.

New Sweden was a different place under Nikolas's rule. The warriors still held steadfastly to the old ways, but women had gained more freedoms and rights. At times it had been teeth-grittingly slow going, but it had happened and continued to evolve. Nikolas was a just, fair ruler. He held his people together with a reasonable but firm fist.

Ronda had been, uncharacteristically for women down here, vocal in her opinions. She and Nikolas had taken some flack for it over the years, but her popularity amongst the people, especially the matriarchs, was too powerful for a few naysayers to destroy.

Nikolas had turned out to be everything Ronda could ever have wanted in a man and then some: an excellent father who placed as much value on their daughter as he did on their three sons, a wise leader of their people, a thoughtful, loving husband, a fierce warlord, and in a few short weeks when their daughter, Cora, gave birth, she knew he'd be the world's most devoted grandfather, as well.

On most subjects Nikolas was pretty flexible, as Viking warriors went, but on the issue of remaining below the ground his opinion could not be swayed. He clung steadfastly to the belief of the ancients, that one day the inventions of Outsiders would cost them dearly and spread disease and chaos to all those living above the ground. Females, for reasons unknown, would dwindle in numbers and bloodlines would die out.

Ronda could only sigh and shake her head at such alarmist, head-to-the-hills reasoning, but these beliefs were the very foundation of the Underworld culture. She supposed if this belief system ceased to exist, the clans of New Sweden, New Norway, and New Daneland would also cease to thrive.

"Good morn, my loves." Nikolas bent down and kissed Ronda and then their daughter, who were sitting in the solarium. It was the brightest of all the chambers in the Ericsson dwelling, having the most peepholes leading up to the world that lay above. The sun's light shone through strongly in here.

Ronda smiled. "Good morning? It's almost time for dinner. At last, he arises!"

God, he was handsome, she thought, a twinkle of contentment in her eyes. The years had only made him look impossibly better to her. He was as muscled, powerful, and strong as ever. A few laugh lines around the eyes and his salt-and-pepper hair were the only hints he'd aged at all.

"I thought the elders of the council would never cease their prattling last eve. What have you two been doing?"

"Going over plans for the soon-to-be baby's bedchamber," Cora excitedly informed him. "But somehow we got on the subject of how you and mother met." Cora grinned, her father's dimple denting one cheek. "Tell me, did she really knee you in the—"

"Aye," Nikolas cut in, frowning. "I walked funny for days."

As the three of them shared a good laugh over that, Ronda winked at her husband. No matter the gruff voice, she knew he loved that memory. She had been the only person who'd been able to physically thwart him, if even for just a couple of minutes.

"I'd better go," Cora sighed, standing up. Her belly was so ripe Ronda wouldn't be surprised if she gave birth to twins.

"Olaf and I are to sup with his parents this eve."

"Fun, fun," Ronda teased her daughter.

Cora frowned. "If Olaf's sire tells another boring ode of his warrior days gone by, I will throttle him."

"Ahhh," Nikolas chastised his eldest child, "leave Otrygg to his musings. At his age, 'tis all he has left."

Cora smiled her agreement as she lifted her satchel and prepared to leave. "Oh!" she said, looking back at her parents. "I almost forgot to show you something my husband wanted you to see, Papa."

Nikolas lifted one dark eyebrow as Cora fished out an aboveground newspaper and handed it to him. "I don't know how I could forget something like this," she said. "One of Olaf's scouts retrieved this from the Outside." She took a deep breath. "Alas, the prophecy of the ancients is coming to pass. Olaf thought you would want to know before the rest of the Underground is abuzz."

Frowning, Ronda stood and read the newspaper by her husband's side. She stilled, the article jarring:

One year ago today, after twenty-five years of research, scientists perfected the ability to choose the gender of babies to be conceived. Detractors, including many feminist groups as well as the pope, are trying to get genetic tampering barred in Congress, so far with no success. The detractors cite statistics from last year's pregnancies, which suggest that for every female that was born last year, ten male babies had been born . . .

Ronda felt dizzy. Was it true? Could those old prophecies she'd thought of as rubbish actually be coming to pass? Goose bumps formed on her arms.

"Have no fear, my love," Nikolas murmured, sensing his wife's distress. "The Underground is safe." He wrapped a secure, powerful arm around her. That vein-roped arm was as comforting now as it had been two decades ago. "And we always will be."

A smile of admiration and love formed on Ronda's lips. "No matter what lies ahead for any world, above or below the ground, I will always be by your side." She leaned into him, needing his strength and warmth. "I love you, Nikolas Ericsson. I will always love you."

"I love you too, Ronda Ericsson." He waited for her to look up at him, then he winked. "I've always thought you to be very cool."